# The Troll of Newburg

## A FAIRYTALE FOR ALL AGES

### Tony Foglio

WestBow
PRESS
A DIVISION OF THOMAS NELSON

WestBow Press books may be ordered through booksellers or by contacting:

WestBow Press
A Division of Thomas Nelson
1663 Liberty Drive
Bloomington, IN 47403
www.westbowpress.com
1-(866) 928-1240

ISBN: 978-1-4908-0498-9 (sc)
ISBN: 978-1-4908-0499-6 (hc)
ISBN: 978-1-4908-0497-2 (e)

Library of Congress Control Number: 2013916205

Printed in the United States of America.

WestBow Press rev. date: 9/18/2013

# Table of Contents

# Introduction

This is a story about every child's imagination—your imagination. It takes place in the early twentieth century, in about 1910. It is a fairy tale—a fantasy. However, the places are real and so are the people. I have altered the names to add a touch of mystery, or just in case someone does not like his or her character. The house is real, including the three doors. Maybe it's your house, your hometown, or your family. Maybe it's your name I have changed in our story. Even Gillo, the troll, is real. At least he was real to my youngest grandson. The only contrast between his imaginary friend named Gillo and the Gillo of our story is that his friend Gillo was just about always in trouble. When my grandson was about the age of Sue in our story (four), he came walking into the living room with peanut butter all over his face. His mom said, "Didn't I say to stay out of the peanut butter?"

He immediately said, "Yes, but you don't understand; Gillo fell into the peanut butter jar, and I was just trying to get him out." Imagination is an excellent gift. One of the world's greatest minds, Albert Einstein, said it well: "If you want your children to be intelligent, read them fairy tales. If you want them to be more intelligent, read them more fairy tales."

Welcome to Newburg, my hometown.

# ⟫ Prologue ⟪

When you finally go back to your old hometown,
You find it wasn't the old home you missed but your childhood.
—Sam Ewing

Newburg is a gem of a town. Quartz and semiprecious stones were once mined here. It is located on the Moon River, about forty miles west of Mill's Fort, where the north- and south-flowing rivers merge and form the Moon. The town has a fairy-tale appearance, and most consider it to be a friendly place.

A pharmacy and a hardware store are located on Main Street, along with several small shops. Main Street is unusually narrow and only two blocks in length. There are churches on just about every corner, and on Sunday mornings, their bells and chimes compete with hymns of old. There are almost as many taverns, even though they are closed on Sundays.

The streets and the few sidewalks outside of the town center are paved with reddish-brown bricks once fired in local kilns. Many of the old Victorian and Georgian houses along the river are topped with ornate rooms called "widow's watches." These small-windowed rooms were originally atop the homes of riverboat captains, pilots, and engineers. The wives and mothers of these boatmen would anxiously watch for the landing of their husbands and sons.

Newburg is a northern town and borders both the East and the Midwest; therefore, it experiences, in the fullest, all four seasons.

Grace, Hensley, and Sue Addison are fairly new to Newburg. They arrived by train with their mother in late spring last year. Their mom, Mary Addison, was raised near Newburg. She married and moved to the Golden State a little over fifteen years ago, but she has returned as a single mom to be near her extended family. Mary is the only daughter of retired Doctor Joseph and Cora Cola. Doctor Cola and Cora live at 221 Luna-Vista Avenue, in the old Wilson Manor, which was built before the presidency of Abraham Lincoln, circa the early to mid-1800s.

Grace, the eldest daughter of Mary, is sixteen; Hensley is eight; and Sue is four. The Wilson house is a large Georgian[1] with a Florentine[2] courtyard, a vineyard backyard, and a whimsical carriage house where the children's great-grandfather and great-grandmother live. Mary and her children now live with the doctor and Cora.

The children call their grandfather Joseph "Doctor" and their grandmother Cora "Grammy." They refer to their great-grandfather as "Captain" and their great-grandmother as "Great-Gram." John Jaeger was one of the last stern-wheel captains. He and Great-Gram are now in their nineties, filled with wisdom, knowledge, and kindness. The captain is tall and slender and as strong as he was in his river days. He can tell the most far-fetched stories and make them as believable as the Bible. He passes the summer days by splitting firewood and making the children

---

[1] Characteristic of the reign of the British kings George I–IV (1714–1830).

[2] Relating to Florence Italy.

laugh. Great-Gram is as busy as if she were in her twenties. They are a wonderful reflection of Abraham and Sarah of old.

The good doctor is stern but has a tender heart for his family. Cora, Grammy, is the hub of Wilson Manor. She moves with a peaceful swiftness. She can make a meal appear as if by magic. One might think that a myriad of servants staffs the house, but there is not a one. She teaches the children with patience.

## Wilson Manor

There is a garden in every childhood,
an enchanted place where colors are brighter,
The air softer, and the morning more fragrant than ever again.
—Elizabeth Lawrence

The Wilson house is more of an estate home than a city house. All the homes on Luna-Vista are stately. The original house had no bathrooms, and a fireplace heated each room. Sometime in the late nineteenth century, the owners added gas lamps and then, in the beginning of the twentieth century, electricity. There are four large bedrooms and two baths on the top floor. Therefore, there should be six doors to the six rooms, but there are seven. We'll talk of the seventh door later. The main floor consists of two parlors,[3] a large, formal dining room, a bath, and the doctor's library. In the rear of the house is a family drawing room heated with a Franklin stove. There's a galley kitchen and also a large family kitchen with a great cooking fireplace at the west end. Adjacent to the drawing room is a multiwindowed room referred to as "the Tuscan Room" (due to its Italian influence), which overlooks the Florentine courtyard. The front porch is large and requires so much cleaning that Grammy Cora refers to it as "the Veranda Room." There are fifteen rooms in the main house.

---

[3] A sitting room in a private house.

Other than the bathrooms and the mudroom, each room has a fireplace.

The basement was dug after the house was built to install a coal-burning furnace. In the nineteenth century, people, as a whole, were not as tall as they are in our day. Therefore, the basement ceiling is not terribly high. Anyone entering it has to stoop to not bump his or her head on the beams. There is a sign at the bottom of the steps that reads Mind Thy Noggin.[4]

The doctor built a research lab in the lower cellar, where coal was once stored. It is off limits to the children. He is steadily working on research projects, primarily to improve medications for heart disease. He makes wine.

The house has floors so creaky that they speak to all who walk on them. There are secret rooms and numerous hiding places. The main entrance opens into a long foyer and staircase. An eight-foot grandfather clock stands guard, ringing out quarter hours with the chimes of Westminster Abby. If the house were not so filled with guests and children, it would be a ghostly place.

The front-porch view of the river is separated by Luna-Vista Avenue, a perfectly straight brick street, and a grassy slope that runs to the west bank of the river (where the children toboggan[5] during the snows). The Moon River is nearly a mile wide. The beauty of the river alters with the season. The summer frames her it with the greenest of trees. The colors of fall are perfectly mirrored in her often smooth-as-glass flow. She naps during the gloomy, dark shadow of winter and swells her banks and rushes

---

[4]  A person's head.

[5]  To ride a long, narrow sled used for the sport of coasting downhill over snow or ice.

Page 4

in torrents during the spring. When the air is crisp and moist and the river is calm and warm, a haunting mist covers her like a feathery quilt. The Moon River, as said by many, "is a dream maker, alive with wonder."

The house is surrounded by brick pathways that meander through various bench-strewn flower and Terracotta-pipe[6] gardens designed just for dreaming and wondering. Captain John defines them jokingly as "places where I sometime sits and thinks and other times I just sits." As the house is far from square, there are various coves and decks hidden from view. No matter which way you wander, every path leads to the Florentine courtyard and then to Captain John and Great-Gram's carriage house, the pavilion, the play yard, and the doctor's vineyard. If ever there were an estate that loved children, the Wilson Manor is it.

---

[6] Clay-based, unglazed ceramic pipes used as planters and ornaments.

# —➤ Chapter 1 ✦—
# When Stories Begin

Sweet dreams of flying machines, pony rides, and all happy things.
—The Author

t is the time of year when days are long and nights are sultry. School is a distant memory. Friendships are settled, countless ball games have been played, and parents are ready for summer to end and school to begin again.

Incandescent[7] streetlights are new to Luna-Vista Avenue—corrugated porcelain lampshades held by what look like shepherds' crooks. Days now linger into the dark of night with the advent of the electric streetlamp. The children, sticky and sweaty, sit on the street curb, reminiscing over their long day of play, all talking at the same time while mosquitoes and moths cast shadows in the glow of the hanging lamps.

The children look into the star-filled sky. They see a shooting star and make a wish. It is an unusually clear night due to a rare breeze from the east. Typically, the stars are not visible due to the

---

[7] An electric light containing a filament that glows white-hot when heated by an electric current.

constant smoke from the coke[8] ovens and the coal-fired power plant that are located both north and south of Newburg.

"Hensley! Sue! Mom says it's time to come in!" shouts the sweet sixteen-year-old Grace.

"Aw, Grace, can you ask her if we can stay out just a little longer? All the kids are here!"

"No! She says come in right now; you have to take your baths and eat dinner."

Hensley, being eight, is somewhat embarrassed that he and Sue have to go in, when most of the other kids who are younger than he, some as young as Sue, get to stay out. Little does he know that many of the children will go to homes less pleasant than his. Since the mines and refineries closed, many of the families in Newburg are hurting and have a hard time even feeding their children.

When Hensley and Sue walk into the house, Grammy Cora shouts, "Stop right there! Take off those muddy shoes and dirty clothes before you take another step." There is nothing more humiliating for an eight-and-a-half-year-old boy than taking his clothes off in front of girls.

Hensley is a towheaded, straight-backed, slim, and handsome boy. He seems to begin most of his sentences with "Aw, Grammy" or "Aw, Mom" when speaking to either Grammy Cora or Mary, his mom.

Four-year-old Sue is totally indifferent. Without breaking stride, she kicks off her shoes and sheds her clothes to the bareness. She laughs, spins, and starts singing an unrecognizable song. Grace, forgetting that she was exactly like Sue when she was Sue's age, indignantly turns to her mom and says what all teenage girls say when they don't know what to say: "Mom!"— which, in this case, means, "Don't let her run through the house naked! What if one of my friends comes over?"

---

[8] A high-carbon fuel made by baking coal in giant ovens.

Grammy and Mary just smile, and Mary says, "Take your brother and sister upstairs for a bath."

Grace responds, "Mom!"

A shout comes echoing down the stairs: "Aw, Mom, come on! Do I have to take a bath with Sue?"

"No, let her go first, and then you," she answers. With relief, Hensley waits in his room, reading the Eclectic Readings'[9] *The Last of the Mohicans.*[10] Sue splashes and sings while Grace attempts to wash her hair, getting as wet as Sue.

Hensley, thanks to Grammy Cora, is a reader like the doctor and her. Each morning during the school year, Grammy and Hensley take turns reading everything from biographies of George Washington to the *Memoirs of Sherlock Holmes.*[11] Little Sue, thanks to the doctor, colors and paints, plays hide-and-seek, and sits atop the library ladder, asking her grandfather about everything in the room. And the library does have just about everything in it: from ancient maps to numerous old books, a pith helmet to a wall covered with photos and artwork. He calls them his treasures.

Grace, like her mother, Mary, has a charm about her, even though she is just a budding, lanky teenager. Mary's work often requires her to travel, leaving Grace to help Grammy Cora with not only the children but also the whole household. Grace takes on these tasks without complaint. She's an honors student about to begin her final year of high school. These teen years are filled with everything from growing pains to decisions about the approaching future. Her thoughts of college weigh heavily on her: *Where shall I go; what shall I be?*

When the baths are over, the children don their pajamas. Grace comes down to help set the table. Hensley comes down

---

9 Stories derived from other works.

10 Hensley is reading an adaptation of J. F. Cooper's *The Last of the Mohicans,* written by Margaret N. Haight in 1909.

11 By A. Conan Doyle.

next, with Sue right behind him, holding the railing and singing a different note with every step. The doctor had taught Hensley that when ascending a set of stairs, the ladies go first, and when descending, the gentlemen go first.

"Why, Grandfather?" Hensley had asked.

"In case the lady stumbles or trips, you are there to protect her—chivalry, my boy, chivalry," he had answered.

Dinner is a joyful time in the Cora Cola kitchen. There are no fixed seating arrangements. The doctor seems to sit in a different place every night. He's usually the first seated. Grammy Cora is always last—and then only at the doctor's calling. There is always a lot of chatter until the doctor grabs the hand next to him, and then everyone grabs a hand. The doctor asks, "Who would like to pray?"

Little Sue is most often the first to respond, "I will! I will!" Unless the doctor asks someone else, she immediately begins her homily.[12] Her little legs start to kick quickly back and forth in a joyous blur as she begins to pray. With eyes wide open, she prays, "Thank you for Grammy, Grandfather, Mommy, Sissy, Hensley, Bo" -the dumbest dog this side of the Mississippi- "Great-Granddaddy Captain John, Great-Grammy, the trees, the table, and our spoons and forks ..."

Sue continues to list whatever she sees until Mary says, "Sue."

She then—and only then—closes with "Okay, Mommy, and the food. Amen."

---

[12] A religious discourse that is intended primarily for spiritual edification; a sermon.

## — Chapter 2 —
# The Mysteries of a Stormy Night

Every [child's] life is a fairy tale, written by God's fingers.
—Hans Christian Andersen

fter dinner, the children are ready for bed—well, the adults are ready for them to go to bed. "It's Saturday night, and church is in the morning. Early to bed and early to rise makes the children healthy, wealthy, and wise," says Grammy Cora.

Mary goes into Sue's room (the room Sue shares with Grace) and says her prayers with her. Sue asks every question she can think of, naturally, to not have to go to sleep. Then Mary goes into Hensley's room for the same. "Now I lay me down to sleep, I pray the Lord my soul to keep. If I should die before I wake, I pray to God my soul to take."[13]

The doctor and Grammy Cora walk from room to room, telling the children, "Good night, don't let the bedbugs bite." That's just one of the silly things grandparents say.

Hensley appeals, "Grandfather, can I ask you a question?"

"Sure, what is it, Hensley?" returns the doctor.

"Why is it that when I pray at night, we say, 'If I should die before I wake'? That's a terrible thing for a little boy to say before

---

[13] From the *New England Primer*, the first reading primer for the American colonies, published in the eighteenth century.

he goes to sleep. Who wants to go to sleep with waking up dead as the last thing on his mind?"

Sometimes children can ask questions that cause adults to have the strangest looks on their faces. "Well, Grandfather?" Hensley echoes.

"Hensley, that's a good question. How about we talk about it tomorrow?" The doctor turns to walk out of the room, and all of a sudden, there's a bright flash and a rumbling kaboom! The breeze from the west has brought in a late-summer storm complete with wind howling, trees hitting against the house, rain blowing sideways, bright flashes of lightning, and booming claps of thunder. "Grandfather," Hensley says with a higher pitch in his voice, "can I ask you another question?"

Grammy and Mary quickly make their way to Sue and Grace's room. A thunderstorm has a way of bringing out the little girl even in a sixteen-year-old young lady. The older people are comforting the little people, but if the adults are honest, they are just as frightened, except they have to put on their brave.

The doctor fondly turns to Hensley. "What is it, my boy?" asks the doctor, understanding that it will be hard for an imaginative eight-year-old to fall asleep in this thunderstorm.

"Grandfather, I was wondering—are there not six rooms upstairs?"

"Well, let's see," he said, counting in his head. "Yes, that's right. There are six rooms."

"Then why are there seven doors in the hallway?" Hensley asks, not wanting the doctor to leave just yet.

## The Three Doors

The doctor sits on the edge of the bed and begins a longer answer than Hensley expected. "Well, my boy, when we bought the Wilson house, I asked the previous owner the same question.

I remember his answer very well. More than his answer, I remember the almost frightened look on his face as I asked. It was as if he were searching for an answer he neither had nor desired to give. Now, mind you, there is nothing mysterious about that door, but there isn't a clear answer either. Nevertheless, here's what he told me: 'The door,' the gentleman said, stammering, 'isn't a real door; it's just there for architectural detail.' He answered as if asking the question himself. The look on my face obviously asked for an additional explanation. 'This end of the hallway,' he said, 'is called the *Alice in Wonderland*[14] keyhole.' I'm sure the questioning look on my face expressed even more wonder. He went on: 'It's there just to balance out the quadrant[15] of the space and the hexagon[16] ceiling window.'"

Hensley, with a look of confusion, says, "Oh?"

"I've tried to open it several times without any luck. So I'm pretty sure it is as he said," replies he doctor. He then pats Hensley on the head, gives him a kiss on the forehead, and gets up to leave.

Hensley—still not ready for sleep—asks as the doctor is almost out of the room, "Are there any other doors that won't open?"

The doctor hesitates for a moment and then returns to the room. "Well, now that you asked, buddy, there are a couple of other doors that either will not open or are not to be opened," says the doctor. "In Grammy Cora's and my room, there is a wardrobe closet; it is kept locked."

"Why?" asks Hensley, wide-eyed with wonder.

Grandfather again sits on the edge of the bed and says, "You know that there are things for children, and there are things for adults. And there are things for both adults and children.

---

[14] 1865 novel written by English author Charles Lutwidge Dodgson under the pseudonym Lewis Carroll.

[15] Each of four parts of a space.

[16] Having six straight sides and angles.

Grandfather keeps the wardrobe locked so that young, inquisitive minds will not open it. In it are things that are not only valuable to Grammy and me but also locked for safety. Grammy keeps some jewelry that was given to her by her mother and from me. I also keep an old gun that my father gave me, and his father gave him. Little Sue would, I'm sure, love to play with Grammy's jewelry. She wouldn't understand that it is not like the costume trinkets that your mom and Grammy let her play with. The same is true with that old gun. It's not like your toy guns; it's a real gun and is very dangerous. Even though I know that you would never play with it, it is best kept under lock and key. Do you understand, my little buddy?"

Hensley nods with a somewhat questioning "Yes." Hensley then asks, "And the third door, Grandfather—the third one?"

"You know, it's getting late, and we have church tomorrow," replies the doctor.

"Grandfather!" cries Hensley. "You can't leave a kid now! You've got to tell me about the third door or … or I won't be able to sleep a wink."

"Your mom and Grammy aren't going to be happy with me, keeping you up this late."

*Crack, bang* echoes the thunder, and *flash, flash* again zips the lightning. Hensley is now sitting up in bed and sitting as close to his grandfather as he can.

"Okay, buddy, I'll tell you about the third door, but it will have to be our secret."

"Cross my fingers, Grandfather—cross my fingers! It will be our secret—honest!" Hensley excitedly answers.

"You know the old silver maple tree next to the grotto?" asks the doctor. Hensley nods. "Anyway, it's a very old tree, and it is hollow."

"Hollow?" asks Hensley.

"Yes, hollow; that means that inside that old tree is just a big, empty space."

"Why? How?" asks Hensley, wide-eyed.

"Trees become hollow when the center of the tree decays. This doesn't mean that the tree is dead or even that it will die. The living part of the tree is found just beneath the bark. Hollow trees can be caused by many things, especially when they get old."

"Like what?" Hensley interrupts.

"Sometimes disease or, like tonight, rain and lightning. Anyway, that old tree is hollow."

"Okay, but what does that old tree have to do with the third door?" asks Hensley.

The doctor answers, "You know in front of the tree is a thick, prickly rosebush?"

"Uh-huh," Hensley says, nodding.

"I was out pruning the courtyard the other day, and while I was trimming that rosebush, I noticed that behind it—at the bottom of the maple tree—was, of all things, a miniature door."

"A door? What kind of door? Why would there be a door?" interrupts Hensley.

"Wait a minute, buddy—wait a minute. I'm not sure why. I've tried to open it, but like the seventh hallway door, I couldn't. It was clearly an extremely old door; it looked as old as the tree itself. It had a small brass doorknob and keyhole, but no key that I had would unlock it. How about I show it to you tomorrow? Remember, it will be our secret—okay?"

"Okay, Grandfather," says Hensley sleepily. It is getting awfully late, and Hensley is ready to go to sleep.

"Good night, my little buddy."

"Good night, Grandfather."

After giving his grandson a smile and another kiss on the forehead, the doctor leaves the room.

The storm lightens up to a mild, steady summer shower. As everyone is either asleep or falling asleep, the muffled whistle of a passing train harmonizes with the falling rain. I'm sure you can imagine the dreams of the children—probably just like dreams that you might have had on a rainy night.

## Sunday

The smell of bacon and buckwheat[17] pancakes fills the morning air. (I think that the smell of bacon in the morning could even tempt angels.) As always, Sue is the first child awake. Grammy Cora and Mary have already had their coffee and, along with Grace, are busy in the kitchen with Sunday morning breakfast. The doctor is in his library, reading his devotionals and, as always, the Bible. Breakfast is at 8:15 sharp. No one is ever late for a Sunday morning breakfast of buckwheat cakes, bacon, sunny-side-up eggs, homemade jam, biscuits, and maple syrup from Paul and Mary, their delightful neighbors. The sun is shining through the thinning clouds, and the air is crisp and has the fresh smell of the wet ground. Put it all together, and it makes the best of memories.

The family cleans and polishes their shoes, presses their shirts and blouses, brushes their teeth, and combs their hair, and off to church they go. In those days, churches didn't have parking lots. Just about everyone walked to church. In Newburg, most folks attend the church that is in their neighborhood. And just about every denomination is within walking distance. Walking to church is a family affair. No one is in a hurry, and no one is late. Even though there isn't assigned seating, everyone sits in the same place. The choir sings, then the congregation sings, an offering is received, the pastor preaches the sermon, and then the church members are off to Sunday school. Grammy Cora and the doctor attend a class called the "Pairs and Spares." It was once called the "Marrieds' Class," and many years before that, it was the "Young Marrieds' Class." Grace is off with the teens. Sue goes

---

[17] Flour for pancakes or cereal.

to the preschool class, and Hensley to the primary class. If there is a group of saintly people, it has to be Sunday school teachers.

Hensley is always amazed at the stories told in Sunday school: Noah and the ark, David and the giant Goliath, Daniel in the lion's den, and all the various Bible stories. This particular Sunday, the teacher teaches about Noah and the ark. For the sake of discussion and to get the children to think about the lesson, she asks, "Do you think Noah did a lot of fishing, being he was on the seas for over a year?"

Hensley thinks and then answers, "No, ma'am."

"Why not, Hensley?" she asks.

"Well, because he only had two worms."

Before the teacher has time to respond, the church bell rings, and class is dismissed.

The family has Sunday lunches midafternoon, so after church, they stop at the ice-cream parlor at the pharmacist's for an ice-cream sundae. Sue asks Grammy Cora, "Why is ice cream called sundaes on Sundays?"

Grammy looks at the doctor for the answer. The doctor says, "Sue, it's a complicated thing. There are rules called Sunday blue laws.[18] Being that it is the Lord's Day, the stores—and especially the taverns—are to be closed. The drugstores are permitted to be open so folks can get their medications if needed. Most drugstores have soda fountains. The law says that sodas and ice-cream cones should not be sold on the Lord's Day. So they serve ice cream covered with things like fruit and nuts, supposedly making it a health issue. So they call ice cream served this way a sundae." The whole family stares at the doctor in disbelief. He looks back at them and simply says, "And that's the way it is. Let's eat some ice cream."

Sunday afternoon is a time of rest and relaxation. About the

---

[18] Laws that many states upheld to assure religious standards—particularly the observance of a day of worship or rest—that go back to the founding of the country.

only work done is in the kitchen. The doctor has the family sit around the gramophone[19] to listen to his favorite music—which sure isn't the favorite of the children. After lunch, the children are free to play, and the adults rest.

## The Little Green Door

As soon as he is allowed, Hensley runs out the door and heads toward the old maple tree. He carefully squeezes behind the thorny rosebush and brushes away some leaves and twigs. Sure enough, there it is—a small greenish wooden door with a brass doorknob and keyhole. "Wow! Look at that," he says quietly to himself. The old maple tree has a swing attached to one of its strong branches. Hensley sits on it, slowly pushing back and forth and wondering about the strange little door. *What could it be? Why is it there? Who or what built it?*

Sue comes running over. "My turn, Hensley—my turn." Hensley relinquishes the swing to his sister and, deep in thought, walks around the courtyard. Grace comes out, and Sue shouts, "Push me, sissy—push me!"

It is a beautiful Sunday afternoon, but Hensley keeps wondering about that small greenish door in the old maple tree. *What is it? Does it have anything to do with the seventh door upstairs? What is in Doctor's wardrobe? Why didn't I ever see or know about this little odd colored door before? Why did my grandfather say that it was a secret? I wonder,* he thought. *I just wonder.*

Grace continues to push Sue on the swing as they sing a song they learned that

---

[19] Record player by which the sound of a vibrating needle would be amplified.

morning in Sunday school. The three McCartney girls who live behind the vineyard come over to play. The girls are close in age, less than four years apart, the youngest being seven. Hensley enjoys playing with them, even though they are girls. Eight-and-a-half-year-old boys aren't fond of girls, but the McCartney girls can play outdoor games as well as any boy—maybe better. So off they go, through the wicket gate, running and laughing. Sue is soon on their tail, yelling, as all little ones do, "Wait for me! Wait for me!" Several of Grace's friends come by, and with permission (in those days, children did all things only with permission); they walk to the town-square gazebo to listen to a concert by the city band. Sunday afternoons are as good as it gets in Newburg.

After a long day of play, which includes such games as hide-and-seek; Mother, May I?; kick the can; hopscotch; Duck, Duck, Goose; and follow the leader, it is cleanup time for Sunday dinner. On Sundays, the family eats in the dining room. These dinners make for the greatest of family memories. The smells that come from the kitchen, well, they just make your mouth water. It is Grace's job to gather the children and make sure they are clean and tidy. Great-Granddaddy, Captain John, being the family patriarch, sits at the head of the table. The doctor, Grandfather, sits at the other end, and then the adults and children sit in alternating order in the other seats. Discipline and training are always in play. Sunday dinners are led in prayer by the captain. No one asks—not even Sue—if he or she can pray; it is the captain's honor. And boy, can he pray. Every head is bowed, and every eye is closed, for he prays with such a booming voice and with such words that the family members are sure that God is going to appear. And when he says, "Amen," everybody says in his or her loudest voice, "Amen, let's eat!"

The family is blessed to have an abundance for such incredible meals. Momma Mary always teaches the children to be thankful. They rarely have a Sunday dinner without at least one guest. Many times, if not all of the time, the guests are a family whose father has lost a job, or a widow and her children, or, ever-so-often, the pastor and his family. And if there are any leftovers, the family always sends them home with the guests. There is never any leftover pie, but Great-Grammy always walks over to the carriage house and returns with one that she keeps lying around for our guest to take home.

After dinner, the men go (or "retire," as the old folks call it) to one parlor, and the ladies go to the other. The conversation for the gentlemen is mostly about the economy and local and state politics. The ladies speak of domestic issues but also speak about needs in the community, events at church, and education. The children either swing on the front porch, listen to a story read by Grace, or play board games in the Tuscan Room, which is also called the morning room. In all these times, there are never whispers or unpleasant things said about anyone. Everyone leaves the Wilson Manor feeling better about life and him- or herself.

After everyone has gone, Hensley knocks on the library door. The doctor quietly says, "Come in, Hensley my boy; have a seat. What can I do for you this splendid Lord's Day?"

With his feet not reaching the floor, sitting in the old rocking chair between Grandfather's desk and the window, Hensley says, "Grandfather, I saw the little door in the old maple tree today."

"Did you now?" says the doctor with an interrogating voice.

"Yes, sir, and I sure don't know what to make of it. Truth be told, I don't know what to make of a lot of things."

"Like what, son?" the doctor replies in a kindly fashion.

"The seventh door, the locked wardrobe, and now that strange door in the maple tree," says Hensley in an almost grown-up way.

The doctor asks, "Did you tell anyone about the little door?"

"No, sir, you said that it was to be our secret."

"That's good," replies the doctor. "We sure wouldn't want anyone to be worried or frightened about things with no answer, would we?"

"I guess not," says Hensley. "But, Grandfather, what does this all mean? Why would someone make a door that doesn't open, and why is there a door in a tree? And why would you say that the wardrobe also be kept a secret? I've never seen Grammy Cora wearing fancy jewelry. You've always shown me things that your father gave you, and you've never shown me an old gun. We've gone shooting many times. We've hunted rabbits, and I've always had my own 410 shotgun. Grandfather, you have always taught me to speak my mind with honesty and respect. So I'm asking: What do these things mean?"

The doctor sits with his finger tapping his lips, looking up and thinking deeply. He sits up straight, places both feet on the floor, and says, "Ask the captain." Then, after a pause, he says, "Yes, ask the captain. He knows all about these things. He can and will tell you better than I. You're growing up fast, young Hensley—yes, sir, you're growing up fast. I trust that you are mature enough to know the history of the Wilson house and Newburg. Go ahead— go and ask the captain."

## A Lesson in History

The captain is in the pavilion. He has a good fire going and is sitting facing the flames, deep in thought. "Great-Granddaddy," calls Hensley.

"Jumpin' catfish! You about scared the bejeebers out of me, my boy. Don't do that to an old man. I might have taken my last," hollers the captain.

"Sorry, Great-Granddad. But I've gotta ask ya."

"What is it, Hensley?" the captain asks, seeing the boy's concern.

"Grandfather told me last night during the storm about the door to nowhere, the locked wardrobe, and the door in the maple tree. I saw it today. I saw it! I actually saw it—the small little greenish door in the tree, in the old maple tree. I saw it with my own eyes."

The captain pauses and looks up at the tree, which can be seen from the pavilion. "The door—the little door in the old maple tree. I forgot all about that thing. How about that! It's still there. I'll be."

The captain sits quietly for a moment and then slaps his knee and, smiling as if hearing from an old friend, says, "How about that! I'll be! Hensley, my great-grandson, I guess I better tell you the story, for someday, when I leave this good earth, you will be passing it along to your son or your grandson or even your great-grandson. Yes, sir, someday you'll be telling the story. Let me think … Yes, I remember as if it were yesterday. Listen up. Listen carefully.

"Many years ago, I was just about your age. A summer storm came rolling in—kind of like last night's storm. The wind blew wildly, and the thunder rumbled so that the house shook. I was frightened—not as brave as you. That night, the river rose well over flood stage. The old-timers said it was a record. After the storm, some of the neighbor kids and I found a strange little boat atop a tree by the river. Alex Moore and I foolishly climbed that tree, even though it was close to the raging river. We found some rope, and Alex, his older brother, and I lowered the boat to the ground. It wasn't a toy boat, mind you; however, it wasn't a boat that was large enough for regular people. It was a strange vessel yet quite sophisticated. It was made of wood—but a wood that sure wasn't from these parts. It had an ornate hand-carved mast, a brass sundial compass, a couple of strange little books, and three bags of seeds. The bags were in a colorful, unrecognizable fur pouch. The boat was well worn, not so much from the storm but well used, old looking. The furnishings in it were solid, and everything was sculpted with either unusual words or drawings.

"Again, everything was small—but not tiny like Sue's dollhouse furniture." As the captain is telling Hensley the story, it is as if he is reliving it all over again—and to think that it happened nearly ninety years ago. "It was getting late, and the boat was too heavy to carry up the muddy hill. So we tied it to the tree in which it was found and planned on returning in the morning with some help. Well, the river wasn't finished doing its rising. The water was even higher than the night before, and the little boat was gone; it must have come loose and drifted off. It was never seen again.

"Not long after finding that boat, strange things began happening around town. In the middle of the night, dogs would bark and howl and then whimper. Cats would screech and growl like lions. If things were left out of doors and not in their proper place, they would be missing; tools would be in the sheds, toys were in their boxes, and anything that was to be stored was found in its proper place. Maybe the strangest thing was that flowers began disappearing around town—not just any flowers, but roses, and not just any roses, but only white roses like the ones that were once on the bush in front of the old maple tree.

"There was a Mrs. Billingsley, who has long since passed; she was a real horticulturist, and her passion was raising a distinct variety of white roses. Naturally, she was terribly upset at her absconded flowers. One evening, as she was getting ready to retire for the night, she happened to look out her parlor window, and there in the moonlight, she thought that she saw a small boy—an unusually small boy—in her rose garden. He turned toward her and, in an instant, disappeared. She simply thought that it was her imagination and that she was seeing things. However, the next morning, not a rose was left—not a one. Many other strange things were happening around Newburg. Back then, I was just a young lad. Did I say that I was about your age?"

"Yes, Captain, you did," replies Hensley. "What kind of things?" Hensley asks.

"Maybe some of the strangest things were that if any doors were left unlocked, whether accidentally or purposefully, in the mornings, those doors would be found mysteriously locked. There are even tales that—you may not believe this one—doors would be found where there were no doors."

Hensley interrupts, "What do you mean, Great-Granddad?"

"Well, my boy," the captain, almost in a whisper, answers, "I sure don't wish to frighten you, but in your house, upstairs, how many rooms are there?"

Hensley, with a lump in his throat, answers in a shaky, whispery voice, "Six."

"And how many doors are there?" asks the captain.

Hensley, wide-eyed, answers, "Seven! Who did it, Great-Granddaddy—who would do such a thing? How could someone build a door without anyone seeing or hearing them do so? Why? What good is a door that will not open? What is behind our door? Are there others?"

"Slow down, my boy—slow down," says the captain, placing his mighty hand gently on Hensley's shoulder, aware that the boy is getting a bit frightened. There are a few others; Paul and Mary, your neighbors, have one. The Joneses down the street have one. There's one in the old Moore barn and the little one in the old silver maple. I think a couple others, but I just don't remember where. It was the talk of the town for years; people used to travel to Newburg just to see a door to nowhere, a door that didn't open. It sure was a strange thing, I tell you— certainly a strange thing. Furthermore, to this day, some ninety years later, there's not a white rose to be found within the whole county. No, sir, not a single white rose."

"Hensley! Hensley, it's time to come in!" calls Momma Mary.

"Okay, Mom. Good night, Captain."

"Good night, my boy; I'll see you tomorrow."

Evenings before bedtime in their house are most likely the

same as in yours. Everyone goes about his or her evening routine. Mom puts things away and picks up after the little ones. Lights are lowered, doors and windows checked. Grace is still in the bathroom (when you're sixteen, half of life seems like it's in the bathroom). Sue decides it's time to play hide-and-seek with grandfather. Her mom lets her know, in no uncertain terms, it's time for bed. Hensley is quiet this evening, pensive. After what seems to be hours, all the children are tucked in bed. Grace is reading a magazine. Sue is singing. Hensley is lying flat on his back with his hands behind his head, staring at the mobile hanging from the ceiling. As happens each night, Mary prays with her children. Grammy Cora and the doctor move from room to room, saying something sweet. Well, Grammy Cora is. Grandfather usually has something that he thinks is funny to say: "Don't let the bedbugs bite," "Early to bed and early to rise makes children healthy, wealthy, and wise," and his favorite, "No stinkers under the covers," to which Grace replies, "Oh Grandfather!"

# — Chapter 3 —
# The Wonder of Dreams

I left the fairy tales lying on the floor of the nursery,
And I have not found any books so sensible since.
—G. K. Chesterton

ensley has a hard time falling asleep. The events of the day and the previous night keep running through his head: *The storm, the locked doors to nowhere, a mysterious wardrobe, the little door, and that small, odd-looking door in a tree—why haven't we spoken of these things before? Why did the doctor say that it was to be a secret? Locked—they are all locked. Nobody, except maybe the doctor, knows what's behind them.* Hensley drifts from wondering to that time when you still think you're awake but you are mostly asleep. It is the time when dreams are their most vivid and your mind crosses over into the realm of fantasy. This night, he dreams that he is alone in the house. He says to himself, "Maybe I should try to open the seventh door and find the key to the wardrobe and see for myself what is in it." In his dream, he succeeds in opening the doors. However, instead of seeing what is in them, each time he opens one of the doors, he finds himself standing outside next to the old maple tree. That is all he can remember of his dream.

There's just something about dreams. They can awaken you in the middle of the night with a certainty that you will never forget them. Nevertheless, come morning, the dream is, at best, a vague memory, if remembered at all.

Morning comes early for Hensley. He's the first kid up. That's important when there are other children in a house. First Kid Up is a high honor. He jumps out of bed, slips on his play clothes, zips into the bathroom, brushes his teeth faster than a flash, combs his hair with a single stroke, washes his face with a splash, slides down the staircase banister (because no adults are looking), and runs into the kitchen, where Grammy Cora is having a cup of coffee with his mother, Mary. "Hi, Mom. Good morning, Gram."

They, in concert, say, "Good morning. Hensley." "There are pancakes on the stove."

Hensley grabs one and rolls it up and is out the door before his mom can say, "Wait a minute."

It's a perfectly beautiful late-summer morning. The sun is shining, birds are singing, and the air is moist and fresh. The neighbors, Paul and Mary, are already working in their yard.

"Morning, Hensley," they shout.

"Morning, Paul. Morning, Mary," he quickly responds. The captain is at the woodpile, splitting wood. The doctor is caring for his vineyard. There's not another kid in sight. Neither the captain nor the doctor notice Hensley. They are focused on the jobs at hand. That's what grown-ups do. When they're busy, a kid seems to become invisible. Hensley stops right between them, each about a horseshoe toss away, and calls, "Grandfather! Great-Granddaddy!"

They look up as if a voice has come from heaven. They give the usual busy-adult response: "Not now, Hensley; I'm busy."

Hensley is determined. "This is very important; I really need to talk to both of you." The doctor sets down his pruning shears; the captain rests his ax and wedge. By then, Hensley is sitting in the pavilion. Like a prince, with authority, he speaks: "Grandfather, Granddaddy, we need to talk."

"What is it, my boy?" leads the captain.

Hensley has their attention. "I need to know—I really need to know."

"What do you need to know?" asks the doctor with a smile.

"Those doors—I need to know the truth about those doors. I couldn't sleep because of them, and when I did fall asleep, I dreamed of them. I asked you, Grandfather, and you seemed either not to know, or you didn't tell me everything. I asked you, Great-Granddaddy, and you gave me a history lesson. I need the truth—the whole truth about the door in the upstairs hallway, the locked wardrobe door, and, above all, that small door in the old maple tree." Hensley sits back, crosses his arms, and takes a stance that says, *I'm willing to wait all day for an honest answer.*

"Well, Captain?" the doctor says. "Since you know far more than I, are you going to tell him what these doors are all about?"

The captain pats his chin and says, "Hmm." He scratches his head and rubs his knees with both hands.

Hensley says, "What? What is it?"

The doctor says, "We don't honestly know. All we do know is what we heard when we were children like you."

Hensley answers, "Grandfather, you mean to tell me that you do not know what is in the wardrobe?"

"Well, yes, Hensley, I know what's in there."

"Then let's start with the wardrobe; why is it locked, and what's in it?"

The doctor, with the appearance of a kid caught with his hand in the proverbial cookie jar, looks toward the captain and says, "Fairly much like I told you—Grammy Cora's few pieces of jewelry and the old gun passed down from my grandfather."

"What else?" asks Hensley.

The doctor hesitates. "If you must know, there is an old compass, some small books, and a tobacco-size fur pouch."

The captain pipes up. "Do you remember the story about the little boat and the things we found in it? Those are the things I found nearly ninety years ago. I gave them to your grandfather so that someday he could give them to you. We sure didn't think the day would come so quickly."

"What about the seventh door? Is it as you say—it just appeared? Why did you tell me that the previous owner said that it was for architect—or whatever that word is?"

"That is the truth; that is exactly what he told me. It was the captain who told me about it just appearing one morning without anyone knowing where it came from or who built it," answers the doctor.

"And the weird little door in the maple tree—what about it? Why is it there?" asks Hensley.

"Captain, I think you need to answer that one," says the doctor.

Hensley opens his eyes wide and, without blinking, looks to the captain with a bewildered expression.

## The Myth of the Troll

The captain ponders for the longest time; he rubs his chin as if searching his mind for a long-ago memory. "Hensley," he begins, "do you remember me telling you about the strange things that took place here in Newburg after finding the little boat in the tree?"

"Yes, sir," Hensley respectfully replies.

"Mind you, now, I've never myself been able to confirm what I'm about to tell you. I've never seen it myself."

"Never seen what?" Hensley anxiously asks.

"The troll—the Troll of Newburg," the captain says with authority.

"A what?" Hensley replies with an astonished look.

"A troll," Grandfather says more loudly. "A *troll*."

Hensley, with a snicker, says, "What the heck's a troll?"

The doctor pipes up. "Don't say 'heck,' Hensley."

"Sorry, Grandfather, but what's a troll?"

The captain clears his throat. "Again, my boy, I've never seen a troll, but the old-timers say that years ago—no, centuries ago—way up in the Northern Hemisphere, there were mythical giants called trolls. They say the name *troll* comes from some Scandinavian word, *trows*, or an Old English word, *trowian*, which means 'to think, trust, or believe.' So if there are such creatures, one must first believe that they are or at least think that there is such a thing. They say that trolls only come out in the dark of night—maybe from twilight to the break of dawn—and are never seen in the full light of day, for if they are visible to the sun, they either crack or shrink. So, they say, there are few, if any, giant trolls anymore, for over the years of trying to hide from people, they often had to travel in the daylight and have become remarkably small—some less than twelve inches in height.

"No one in Newburg has ever seen one in the daytime, but some say that one was spotted years ago during a full moon. Trolls, I'm told, have very distinctive features; because of their exposure to the sun, their faces look old, like mine—filled with cracks and wrinkles. They have wild, bushy hair, very large ears that can be either pointy or round, unusually wide or crooked noses, and only four fingers on each hand and four toes on each foot. They're usually scruffy and somewhat beastly in appearance. They have extremely short legs, even for their small stature. The old-timers also say that even though they are scary looking, trolls are usually of a good nature and shy and easily tricked. They can live to be hundreds of years old. They mean no harm unless you wish them or someone they care for harm. Again, my boy, I've not only never seen one; I'm also not sure there is such a thing. That's my story; that's all that I know about these creatures called trolls."

"What do they have to do with the door in the old silver maple?" asks Hensley, somewhat bewildered.

"Oh, yes, the door. I always thought that Alex Moore might

have put it there as a prank. However, they say that trolls often make their homes in either old fox dens or hollow trees."

"Does a troll live in our tree?" asks Hensley, somewhat taken back. "Never saw one in my near ninety-four years," replies the captain. "Nope, never have had the pleasure," he repeats.

The remainder of the day is uneventful, other than a light afternoon rain. Grace, Sue, and Hensley play Chinese checkers on the front porch. A sixteen-year-old and a four-year-old, with an eight-year-old in the middle, makes for an interesting time of board games. Grace, being a kind and elegant older sister, keeps the peace between Sue and Hensley, making sure the game goes smoothly. They laugh and enjoy the time together, as well as the summer rain. "Look!" cries Sue. "Look—a rainbow."

Hensley looks up at the bow in the sky and asks Grace, "Do you believe that there is a pot of gold at the end of the rainbow, and do you believe in fairies and trolls?"

"No, there's no pot of gold—only in fairy tales. And as for fairies and trolls, what would make you ask such a question?"

Not wanting to reveal the secret that he and the doctor share, he answers, "Oh, I was just wondering if there were such things."

"Only in storybooks," replies Grace.

"Kind of like Santa, the Easter bunny, and elves?" questions Hensley.

Sue, wide-eyed, stands up and says, "They're real. Great-Granddaddy said so."

Grace, wanting to be careful to not steal a little girl's dreams, says, "The captain would know. I think he knows them personally." She smiles. The rain stops, and the day continues as usual—dinner, cleanup, and off to bed.

# The Dream Returns

The night comes early. Hensley, exhausted from the events of the day, falls fast asleep. No sooner is he asleep than he has what proves to be a recurring dream. He dreams about the locked doors. The dream is the same as the one the night before. He dreams that he is again alone in the house. He says to himself, "Maybe I should try to open the seventh door and find the key to the wardrobe and see for myself what is in it." As in the previous dream, he succeeds in opening the doors. Instead of seeing what is behind them, with each opened door, he finds himself standing in the courtyard next to the old maple tree. As before, this is all he remembers of the dream.

# Chapter 4
# When Seasons of Life Change

I had six honest serving men. They taught me all I knew.
Their names were: Where, What, When, Why, How and Who.
—Rudyard Kipling

ummer is winding down. The trees are slowly changing from shades of green to hues of yellow, orange, and red. The sun sets earlier in the southwestern sky, and the clouds thicken with shadows of gray. The river mirrors the colors of autumn in its ripples. The nights become cooler, and people close their windows. The smell of fermenting leaves and the sounds of autumn are in the air. Fair-weather birds begin their migration as the geese honk in a delta formation. The Creator has mixed His pallet.

It's harvest time in the Moon River valley. Grammy Cora, Great-Gram, and Mary are off to the farmers' market, getting ready for the fall canning of everything from apples to zucchini. Hensley gets a new pair of Buster Browns, and Grace gets a new coat and school uniform. Sue gets a bag full of hand-me-downs. Hensley is about to start third grade, and Grace will be a senior at Newburg High. As their mom was, both are honor students.

Not much has been said about the mysterious doors or the Troll of Newburg; everyone is too busy with the events of autumn and the beginning of a new school year.

# School Days

Hensley is small for his age. Most of the other boys are quite a bit taller than he. The third-grade class, taught by Mrs. Elizabeth Young, consists of nine boys and eleven girls. Hensley sits between Jake Brown and Peewee Jonson, two of the roughest and meanest boys in the school. Both have been held back a year and are that much bigger than all the boys in class.

The teasing of Hensley began back on the first day of first grade. Two downright embarrassing things happened. The teacher asked, "Who would like to go to the restroom?" but Hensley thought that the teacher had asked, "Who would like to go to the restaurant?" So Hensley quickly raised his hand and said with a loud voice, "I'd love to go to a restaurant." The teacher didn't correct him in class, and the boys and girls marched to their respective restrooms. When Hensley stepped inside, he stopped and said with a surprised voice, "Hey, this isn't a restaurant; it's a toilet!" Everyone got a good laugh, including the teacher. To add insult to injury, Hensley had on a brand-new pair of trousers— the kind with just an elastic waist and no zipper—and he had them on backward. The teacher, with a red-faced smile, informed him of the mistake. Humiliated, he slithered into one of the stalls to turn them around, not wanting ever to come out. Thus began the teasing of Hensley Addison.

Hensley takes the ribbing fairly well. He discovered early on that laughing at himself made others laugh at him less. Thanks to the training of his mother, he learned that the teasing of others was an attempt on their part to make themselves look better than they were. The captain would say, "It's like profanity; it is a small mind's way of expressing itself forcefully." Hensley takes it all in stride and with lightheartedness. However, there are times that the line is crossed from playful teasing to hurtful cruelty. Jake and Peewee often cross that line, not only with Hensley but also with others in the class, especially the shy and quiet students.

Even though Hensley is physically capable of defending himself, he always does his best to avoid scraps.[20] Jake and Peewee are the bullies of the playground. During games of tag, they push and hit instead of tag, always making it look like an accident so as not to get in trouble with Mrs. Young. They pull the girls' pigtails, take things from the younger children, and do their best to hurt anyone they can. They are just spitefully mean. However, they are only nasty when together; like all cowards, they are seldom aggressive when alone. One day, at recess, Jake and Peewee pushed a little girl to the ground and purposefully stepped on her hand, causing her to cry in pain. Hensley, with just wrath, pushed them off of her, helped her up, and stood his ground, protecting her against their bullying. Peewee, the bigger of the two, rushed toward Hensley to knock him to the ground. Hensley, using a trick he had learned from the captain, stepped to one side, using Peewee's own motion to hurl him face-first to the ground. Jake just stood there wide-eyed and stunned, but not as stunned as Peewee. Hensley became a hero that day to the other children in the class, but an enemy to Jake and Peewee. They threatened to get even with him. Hensley, without a word, returned to the classroom with the others.

Hensley walks about a half mile to and from school. Even though the school is on a main road, Hensley often takes a shortcut through the woods next to the old Moore barn.

It is a typical fall day; leaves are swirling in the breeze, the air is nippy, and the sky is gray. Rays of sunlight are cutting through the clouds like daggers of light. As he walks by the old barn, he hears a door squeaking in the wind and slamming against the siding. The eerie squeaking of the door sounds like screaming banshees.[21] The shadows of the rickety old barn make it even spookier. To calm his nerves, he starts to whistle and

---

[20] Fights or quarrels.

[21] In Irish folklore, a spirit in the form of a wailing woman heard by members of a family as a sign that someone is about to die.

walk a little faster. As he is passing the squeaking door, all of a sudden, something or someone grabs him and pulls him into the darkness of the barn. Scared beyond words, he doesn't even have the breath to scream. The next thing he knows, he is on the ground, flat on his back, with something crushing his chest. Before his eyes can adjust to the dimness of the barn, he hears yelling of the most terrible profanity. When his eyes adjust, he makes out what is crushing his chest—it is Peewee Jonson. Jake Brown is standing over him, swinging the handle of an old rake wildly. Peewee screams, "We'll teach you to make me look bad! We're going to beat you to a pulp and bury you in that pile of manure. No one will ever find you!" Hensley struggles to get free, but Peewee is too heavy. Suddenly, there is a flash of light, and a gust of wind slams the door shut. Instantly, it is darker than midnight. Both Peewee and Jake scream like girls. There is a quick ruckus, and Peewee lets out a shriek and is suddenly hurled off of Hensley. The door flies open as quickly as it closed. Hensley is on his feet. He sees Jake and Peewee stuck headfirst in the manure pile. They pull their heads out of the muck, spitting and coughing. They look up at Hensley and run out of the barn like rats from a terrier.[22] Hensley brushes himself off, having no idea what has just happened.

---

[22] A small dog of a breed for turning out burrowing animals from their lairs.

# ⇒· Chapter 5 ·⇐
# My Mysterious Friend

A friend is one that knows you as you are,
understands where you have been,
Accepts what you have become, and still, gently allows you to grow.
—William Shakespeare

s the sun peeks around the clouds and through the barn door, Hensley hears the whisper of a gravelly voice: "Hensley Addison, are you without hurt?" Hensley's heart is in his throat. "Who's there?" he asks with a shaky voice.

"Is it not I?" the voice responds.

"Who are you? Where are you?" asks Hensley.

"Am I not right here?" the gravelly whisper responds.

"I don't see anyone," Hensley, with wonder, answers.

"Would I not be over here?" says the voice. Hensley steps deeper inside the barn. "Am I standing on these sticks?" questions the whispery, gravelly voice. For some reason, Hensley is not frightened but, rather, is more curious than anything. As his eyes again adjust to the dimness of the barn, there, on top of a pile of rotting wood, he sees what looks like a small statue or maybe a rag doll.

"Do you now see that it is I?" it says.

"Yes. Wh-who, wh-wh-what are you?" stutters Hensley.

"Is not my reason in time to be called 'friend'?"

Hensley slowly moves even closer to the creature. There, atop the woodpile, stands the most unusual creature Hensley has ever seen. It is about eight inches in height; its head is almost as wide as it is tall. It has enormous, round, mouselike ears; a long, round Pinocchio[23] nose; thick hair sticking straight out of its head; and a humongous, scatter-toothed grin. "Do we not believe that those hooligans will not be troubling Hensley Addison any longer?" the little creature says with a snicker.

Hensley, in amazement, answers, "I don't think they'll be troubling anyone anymore."

"Is that not a good thing, Hensley Addison? Is it not time? Must we not be going?" the creature says. With that, it is suddenly gone.

Hensley yells out, "Wait! Don't go. Who are you? What are you?"

Hensley can hear a faint reply echoing as if from inside a deep cavern: "Shall we not meet again, Hensley Addison, when the time is worthy? Do we not say adieu, adieu?"[24]

Hensley, bewildered by what he would later in life refer to as the "Moore Barn Incident," heads home in a scurry. As he runs into the mudroom—short of breath, naturally—the first thing he hears is "Where have you been? We were getting worried." His mother gives him a hug.

"Oh, nowhere—uh, I was just taking my time, uh, with some friends getting home. Yup, I was taking time with a new friend." Hensley answers as if asking a question instead of answering one. The evening is as uneventful as it can be with Sue, Mary, and the rest of the family. The Wilson house seems alive. There is rarely a quiet time unless all are asleep. Before dinner, there is homework, a game or two, and a bath, and then off to bed.

That night, Hensley again dreams that he is all alone in the

---

[23] A fictional character in the 1883 children's novel *The Adventures of Pinocchio*.

[24] Farewell; bye-bye.

house. He says, "I should try to open the seventh door and find the key to the wardrobe and see for myself what is in it." As in the previous dreams, he succeeds in opening the doors. Instead of seeing what is behind them, with each opened door, he finds himself once again standing in the courtyard next to the old maple tree.

Mornings on school days seem to arrive extra early. After breakfast and before heading off for school, Hensley walks out to the courtyard and takes a peek behind the rosebush at the little green door. "There it is," he says to himself. "Hum, there is something different than before. I'm not quite sure what it is, but there is just something different." After a round of hugs and good-byes and a "have a good day," Grace and Hensley are off to school. The high school is just two blocks north up the river, and the grade school is southwest, down the river and on the other side of town nearly a half mile. This morning, Hensley sticks to the sidewalks instead of using the shortcut through the woods and past the old Moore barn.

School is just school that day. When recess comes, Jake and Peewee are reserved and play marbles with a couple other boys. Not a word is spoken about the Moore barn incident.

After school, Hensley bravely decides to take the shortcut through the woods, past the old Moore barn. With his heart thumping and taking easy, quiet steps, looking over his shoulder to see if Jake and Peewee are around, he stops next to the barn. He thinks for a minute and walks up to the door. It is leaning; the top hinge is broken from being slammed the day before by the wind—or at least he hopes it was the wind. He sticks his head in the door and says in a slightly shaky voice, "Hello—is anybody there?" No answer. A mouse runs across his feet, scaring him to a shout and causing him to leap backward out the barn door. Nothing. There is no sign of the little creature he saw—or at least thought that he saw—yesterday.

Hensley gets home on time and goes through the after-school

routine: wash up, change clothes, do homework, and then have dinner. During dinner, Grace's seat is empty. "Where's Sissy?" asks Sue.

"She's not feeling well," her mom answers.

After dinner, Hensley goes up to Grace's room, knocks, and peeks in. "Hi, Gracey. How ya feelin'?" Grace is sitting next to the window with her head resting on her hands, staring at the sky.

"Hey, sis—are ya okay?"

Without looking at Hensley, she says in a soft voice, "I'm okay, little brother. I'm okay." There is something unique between brothers and sisters. It's hard to explain, but there is something special. They can argue and tease, but when there is trouble, they always seem to be there for each other.

Hensley, sensing that something is wrong, asks, "What's wrong, Grace?" Grace puts her face in both hands and sobs. Hensley stands by his sister with his hand on her shoulder. "What's wrong, Grace? Are you sick?"

Grace almost shouts, but in a low voice, "They're just so mean. I've never done anything to make them hate me so. I could just scream. Why do they say such things? What have I done?"

"Who? What? Who hurt you? Who said what things?" asks Hensley.

"The popular girls," she says, making quotation marks with her fingers. "It's one thing not to be part of their little group, but why do they make up lies and ugly stories about others? I've never done anything to them. I'm always polite and friendly. It's okay that I'm not with the in crowd, but why do they like being cruel and demeaning?"

Hensley keeps his hand on her shoulder with eyes wide open, not having a clue what to say. So he says, "Do you want me to hit them with mud balls?"

Grace laughs. "No, little brother, no. I'll be all right. You're the sweetest."

That night, Hensley says a special prayer for his sister—a

prayer that only little boys would make. He prays, "Dear God, my sister feels real bad. Please help her feel better. I hope those girls get the cooties.[25] Amen."

The dream again returns: he is all alone in the house. He says, "I should try to open the seventh door and find the key to the wardrobe and see what's in it." As in each dream, he opens the doors. With each opened door, he finds himself standing in the courtyard next to the old maple tree. But tonight's dream does not end there. In this dream, the rosebush is gone, and there is a clear path to the little door. He looks around; it's foggy. He knocks on the door. It doesn't open, but standing on a branch in the tree is the little creature he saw in the Moore barn. In the distinctive, gravelly voice, it asks, "What can I do for you, Hensley Addison? What can I do?"

"Help my sister," Hensley replies.

"Can I help your sister? Can I if we want to? Should we not say good night, Hensley Addison? Should I not say adieu, adieu?" Morning comes early again.

The day passes quickly: school, the walk home, homework, and dinner. At the dinner table, Grandfather asks how everyone's day went. Most give one-word answers:

"Good."

"Fine."

"Pleasant."

But not so with Grace. She seems to be pensive.[26] "And how about your day, Gracey?" the doctor asks.

Grace puts down her spoon and says, "Well, I'm not sure. I think it was a good day."

"What do you mean you *think* it was a good day?"

"Three of the most popular girls in the school—they are beautiful and pristine—well, they were absent today. The

---

[25] Lice: small, infectious, parasitic insects that live on the skin.

[26] Thoughtful.

principal called for an assembly to inform all the students that there are students with infectious body lice and that they should be careful and take preventive measures not to be in contact with anyone infected. I'm afraid that these three girls have them."

"Cooties! They have cooties! Yahoo! Isn't that great?" shouts Hensley.

"Hensley Addison, that's not a bit nice," says his mother, Mary.

"Nice lice," replies Hensley.

"No. No, my boy, lice can cause various other sicknesses," says the doctor.

Grace says, "I feel so very bad for them."

Hensley, wide-eyed, retorts, "Bad? I thought you'd be glad."

Grace says, "Great-Gram said that the Bible says we are to "Love our enemies, bless them that curse us, do good to them that hate us, and pray for them which spitefully use us, and persecute us.""[27]

"That's right dear," says Grammy Cora. "That's right."

Hensley goes out to the courtyard after dinner. Lo and behold, the rosebush is gone. He runs into the house and into the library and asks the doctor, "What happened to the rosebush?"

"Cut it down," answers the doctor without looking up from what he is reading. "Didn't produce roses anymore, so I cut it down."

Hensley goes back out and thinks, *Just like the dream—it's just like the dream.* He looks up to the branch he saw in his dream and, for a moment, imagines the little creature standing there. He then says in a whisper, "You gave them the cooties. You gave them the cooties. Wow! Thanks."

---

[27] Matthew 5:44

# When Dreams Cross Over into Reality

Mrs. Young's class is studying the poetry of Hans Christian Andersen.[28] Mrs. Young asks the class, "What is the difference between the words *reality* and *feeling*?"

Hensley raises his hand. "My great-granddaddy says that what we feel to be true is often greater than what is really true."

"That's good, Hensley, but what do these words mean by their definition?" she replies.

Connie raises her hand and answers, "Reality is something that we know is true, and feelings are something we think are true?"

"Very good, class; for tonight's assignment, you are to read 'The Tallow[29] Candle.'"

That night, Hensley reads the story with Grace, in case there are words he doesn't understand.

## "The Tallow Candle," by Hans Christian Andersen

It hissed and fizzled as the flames fired the Tallow Candle's mold—and out it came, a pristine solid, shinning, white, slim candle; it was made in such a way that everyone who saw it believed that it had a bright and glowing future. A promise that everyone believed it desired to follow and fulfill.

A fine sheep was the candle's mother, and the melting pot its father. Its mother had given it a bright white body and an idea about life. Its father gave it a longing for flaming that would eventually go through its marrow and bone and shine in life.

That's how it was born and had

---

[28] Nineteenth-century Danish author and poet, 1805–1875.

[29] A hard substance made from animal fat, used in making candles and soap.

grown, and with the best and brightest anticipation cast itself into existence. There it met so very many strange creatures that it desired to learn about life. And maybe find a place where it would fit in. But it had too much trust in the world; a world that only cared about itself, and not at all about the Tallow Candle. It was a world that didn't understand the value of the candle, and therefore used it for its own profit, handling the candle incorrectly; with greasy fingers leaving large stains on its unspoiled white goodness which eventually faded away. It was totally covered with the dirt of the world to which the candle came too close; much closer than the candle could bear. The world was not able to recognize the dirt from its purity—though it remained clean and pure on the inside.

False friends found they could not reach its inner beauty and angrily threw the candle aside as useless.

The blackened outer shell kept all the good people away. They were scared as they would be stained with the candle's grime and blemishes.

So there was the poor, solitary Tallow Candle left alone, not knowing what to do. Rejected by the good, it now realized it had only been a tool of the wicked. It felt so incredibly sad because it had spent its life to no good. It had perhaps stained the better parts of its surroundings. It just could not know why it had been created or where it belonged; why it had been put on this earth—maybe to end up ruining itself and others.

More and more, and deeper and deeper, it contemplated—but the more it considered itself, the more despondent it became, finding nothing good, no real importance for itself, no real goal for the life it had been given at its birth. As if the dirty cloak had also covered its eyes.

But then it met a little flame, a tinder-box.[30] It knew the Tallow Candle better than the candle knew itself. The tinder-box had such a clear view. It could see right through the outer shell, and inside the candle it found so much good. It came closer, and there was brightness inside the candle—it lit and its heart melted.

Out burst the flame, like the triumphant torch of a blissful wedding. Light burst out bright and clear all around, bathing the way forward with light for its surroundings. Its true friends were now able to seek truth in the glow of the candle.

Its body was strong enough to give nourishment to the fiery flame. One drop upon another, like the beginning of creation it trickled down the candle, covering the old dirt with its white stream.

The stream was not just the physical, but also the spiritual realm of the marriage.

And the Tallow Candle had found its proper place in life—and proved that it was a real candle, and went on to shine for many years, pleasing itself and the creation around it.[31]

After they read the story together, Grace says, "You know, little brother, those mean girls, like Jake and Peewee, are just soot-covered candles. They have too much trust in the world,

[30] A metal box for holding a flammable material, flint, and steel for starting a fire; used before matches.

[31] Adapted from "The Tallow Candle" by Hans Christian Andersen, discovered in 2012.

and they are unable to tell the grime from the pure. We need to be a tinderbox to help them see the good that can be found on the inside. Sometimes we too are like the Tallow Candle; we get all smudged with the dirt and grime of bitterness and jealousy. Thanks, Hensley, for sharing your homework with me."

"Sure, Grace," says Hensley.

Grace hugs her brother and says, "Good night, Hensley."

"Good night, Grace; pleasant dreams."

"You too, little brother," replies Grace, throwing a sisterly kiss.

Elizabeth Young is a wonderful teacher. She makes learning not only fun but also something to be desired. Of course, she always says, "When the student is ready, the teacher will come." Hensley is an eager student. He loves to learn just about anything.

"How did everyone enjoy the story of the Tallow Candle?" Mrs. Young asks with excitement, trusting that everyone has not only read the story but also enjoyed it. Yet not everyone did their homework. Some neglected the assignment out of laziness; others had reasons that sometimes are hard to explain or understand. When children would not do well on quizzes or tests, she would always say, "Sometimes there is at least one thing that none of us knows about any given situation. So let us not judge others by what they can or cannot do." She is one of the most patient and understanding people Hensley knows—or will ever know for the rest of his life.

Mrs. Young appears to have eyes in the back of her head, and she seemingly sees things happening even if she is nowhere in sight. She can look at you, and you know she knows what you are thinking. When reviewing the story of the Tallow Candle, she explains the candle and the tinderbox in such a way that everyone knows which one he or she is. She closes the class by asking, "Okay, was the story a reality or a feeling?"

Most answer, "It was only a feeling."

With a smile, she glances at Hensley and says, "Sometimes feelings are the reality. Class dismissed."

## A Fall Saturday

Fall is at its peak. Due to a good and wet summer, the trees are in full color—the reddest of reds, the most brilliant yellows, and colors that cannot be explained. And the smells—there is something about the air in the fall that is unmatched during any other season. Even the freshness of the flowers in the spring cannot match the tangy, fresh air of the fall. The seasons are a metaphor[32] of life. In life, our greatest strengths often become our greatest weaknesses. Fall is like that; the blessing is in the color of the leaves, and the problem is having to rake those same leaves. Raking leaves is a family affair. Everyone is responsible for a portion of the yard. Every Saturday morning, after an early breakfast, is "leaf day." It always amazes Hensley that there are so many leaves on one tree. Grammy Cora and the doctor have a running debate about whether there are more leaves than grains of sand. Grammy is convinced that there have to be more leaves. The doctor puffs up and says in his manliest voice, "Now, Cora, just grab a handful of sand, shake the sand out of your hand, and attempt to calculate the grains that remain—impossible, I say. Impossible." All chuckle as they rake. They always heap the leaves either on the curb of the street or in the garden area and burn them. However, before burning them, there is a time of play. Here's how it goes: "Okay, children, stay out of the leaves. I don't want you spreading them around, and I sure don't want you getting all dirty," says one or all of the adults. No sooner are the words said than either the captain or the doctor grabs the closest child and tosses him or her into the pile of leaves. The laughter is more than contagious. Sue, being the smallest, is usually the first

---

[32] One thing used to represent something else.

thrown, followed by Hensley and even Grace, and if she can be caught, Grandfather tosses Mary in and starts chasing Grammy Cora. None knew she could run so fast. The fondest of memories are being made.

Hensley's area is raking around the old, hollow maple tree. Naturally, his curiosity is on the little green door in the tree. He keeps thinking, *Who would put a door in a tree? How silly is that?* Every once in a while, as he rakes, he bends over and wiggles the tiny knob or shakes the door. He even gets down on his hands and knees and knocks.

The two main trees in the courtyard are the old maple and the American elm. Both are approximately the same age, about 150 years old or older. They are parallel to each other in a north–south line, about fifty feet apart. An old barn owl spends much of the early evenings and mornings in the elm. Owls are the strangest of birds: squatty, with enormous heads and the largest of eyes. It seems as if they can turn their heads entirely around. No matter how many times one steps out into the courtyard in the evenings or early mornings, the "who-o-o, who-o-o" of the owl sends shivers up his or her back. And no matter who it is, they always have something to say to the owl. The look on the owl's face indicates that he knows what you said and that it makes no sense to him whatsoever.

Grace, Mary, Gram Cora, and Great-Gram spend the rest of the day in the kitchen, cleaning and drinking tea and laughing. Great-Granddad and Grandfather are fixing and repairing who knows what. Sue spends most of the afternoon swinging and singing on the old maple swing. Hensley spends most of the day chasing his thoughts. *What a strange week,* he thinks. *The three doors, Grandfather's explanations, the captain's history of the little boat and the Troll of Newburg, the events at school, and then the confrontation with Jake and Peewee in the barn. On top of all that, there was the creature in the barn and the teasing girls getting the cooties. It's been a real strange week, indeed a real strange week.*

Hensley continues chasing his thoughts like a hound chases rabbits. *Was the creature in the barn the Troll of Newburg? Did it give the teasing girls the cooties? Too many questions; not enough answers.* It is too much for an eight-year-old boy to figure out.

That evening after dinner, Hensley goes outside and meanders through the courtyard in his wonders. He can't resist the little green door. He looks around, making sure no one is watching, bends down, and again knocks. He swears he hears, "Who's there?" He stands up again, looking around, expecting to see Grandfather or the captain, joking with him. He looks up into the American elm, and sure enough, there's that old hoot owl. He laughs and says, "You got me again, you old bird. It was you who said 'who-o-o.' Yeah, you got me again." So out of a little frustration, he gives the little door a swift kick. He turns to walk away and hears, "Who's there?"

Again looking around for the prankster and seeing no one, he bends down and says, "Who said, 'Who's there?'"

A familiar gravelly voice answers, "Was it not I who said, 'Who's there?'"

With a frog in his throat, Hensley whispers, "Are you in there?"

The gravelly voice replies, "If I'm not out there, then am I not in here?"

"What the heck?" says Hensley with wonder.

The gravelly voice says, "Are you permitted to say 'heck'?"

"Is that you, Grandfather?" Hensley asks with a chuckle.

The voice answers, "Would the captain be in a tree?"

"Well, no, but neither should I be talking to a tree," Hensley answers as he kneels down and turns his head sideways to peek through the keyhole. "Woo-hoo!" he shouts as he sees another eye looking back at him. "What the heck?"

"Are you not to say 'heck'?"

"Yeah, I know, but what the heck is going on here?" Hensley answers.

"Would it favor you to come visit my home?" the voice asks.

"How? I can't fit through this door; plus, it's always locked," Hensley answers.

"Is it not locked because of doubt?" says the voice.

"That makes no sense," says Hensley.

"Is not doubt the stepsister of unbelief?" the voice answers.

"What?" responds Hensley.

"Is it not so that if you believe, all things are possible to them that believe?"

"I believe that I cannot fit through this little door," Hensley says with frustration.

"Is not there a ladder hanging on the neighbor's fence?" says the gruff voice.

"A ladder? What am I supposed to do with a ladder?" asks Hensley.

"Are not ladders for climbing?" whispers the voice.

"What the heck? I know, don't say 'heck.' But what in the world am I to do with a ladder?" replies Hensley.

"Why not get the ladder? Why not stand it up against the tree? Why not climb it to see?"

"Why not!" says Hensley. So Hensley gets the ladder, awkwardly carries it to the tree, leans it up, checks its sturdiness, and climbs to the fork in the tree, about twelve feet.

"Okay, I'm up the tree. What now?" Hensley asks.

"Can you reach the fork in the tree? Can you step there?" says the one in the tree.

"I'm there; now what?" Hensley shouts down the tree.

"What is there to see?" replies the voice in the tree.

"I can see the neighbors' houses, the river, and the vineyard. I can see a lot of things," says Hensley.

"Under your feet, what can be seen?" responds the voice in the tree.

Hensley looks down at his feet and sees what looks like a piece of roofing slate. "I see a piece of slate," answers Hensley.

"Why not lift it?" says the voice.

Hensley, holding on to a small branch, bends down and attempts to lift the piece of slate. He finds it to be hinged. He raises it up and sees a narrow, ornate set of wooden stairs descending into the tree. The opening is just wide enough for him to climb down. Hensley sticks his head into the hole; the staircase seems unusually long, and at the bottom is a dim light. As if from a great distance, he hears the voice say, "With care, why not climb down?"

"Oh boy! What am I doing?" whispers Hensley. He turns around, feeling with his right foot and then left, and begins his descent down the staircase. As he climbs down, he keeps looking up. The captain has told him, "If afraid of climbing, always look up and it's not as scary." As he continues down, the opening at the top keeps getting smaller and smaller, and the further he descends, the staircase keeps getting wider and wider. After what seems to be an endless descent, he reaches the bottom and steps off of the stairs. He turns around and discovers he's standing in a large foyer, larger than the Wilson house. "What the heck?" utters Hensley.

"Do you not feel welcome?" says the creature in his gruff voice as he approaches Hensley, respectfully bowing his large head. "Am I not honored to have Mr. Addison in my humble abode?" says the little creature that was in the barn.

"Where am I? How'd I get here? Where's the tree? This is very weird," says Hensley in disbelief.

"Would you not like to come sit and have some tea and crumpets?"[33] asks the little being.

Hensley stands there, just gazing in disbelief. "What are you? What are crumpets? What's going on?" Hensley asks, a bit fearful.

"Are you not here because you have chosen to believe? Have you not put aside your doubts, or have you chosen to believe your doubts and doubt your belief?" lectures the little creature.

---

[33] A thick, flat, savory cake cooked on a griddle and eaten toasted and buttered.

"Are you a troll?" asks Hensley, allowing his mind to speak before weighing his words.

"Am I a troll? Is that what you ask? What if I were to tell you that I am? Would you not be frightened?" Hensley does not know whether to laugh, cry, scream, or run up the staircase. "Are you afraid of me? Should I not be afraid of you?" says the troll.

"What are crumpets?" asks Hensley.

"Would you like to try some and see?" asks the troll. Hensley follows the quick, short steps of the troll as the troll keeps looking back at him, saying, "Will you not come? Will you not join me? Will you not make yourself at home?" The troll opens a large set of double doors leading into a vast dining room with murals, a candle chandelier, and a table that would seat a dozen people. "Will you not have a seat? Will you not wait? Will I not get the tea and crumpets?" happily asks the troll.

## Hensley's New Best Friend

Hensley takes a seat at one end of the long table, and the troll brings in a tray of tea and crumpets. The troll climbs up on a full-sized chair and stands at the other end of the table. His head barely clears the top of the table. They drink their tea and eat their crumpets. "How were our tea and crumpets?" asks the troll.

"They were wonderful; I've never had anything better. Even Grammy Cora's chocolate-chip cookies aren't as good. Well, maybe they are as good," says Hensley.

The troll asks, "Would you like to sit by the fire in the parlor?"

"You have a fireplace and a parlor?"

"Should I not have them?" inquires the troll.

"Well, I guess I shouldn't be surprised; there seems to be everything else in this old maple tree," Hensley says laughingly. Hensley follows the troll through a wide hallway into a well-furnished parlor. There is a massive stone fireplace with lion andirons[34] guarding the hearth. In the room, there are a large leather sofa and two leather high-backed armchairs. A tapestry of a strange land hangs on the wall opposite the fireplace. A clear-as-crystal table sits in the middle of the room, with large books containing unfamiliar words and pictures on their covers. The troll invites Hensley to take a seat: "Would you have a seat, my friend Hensley Addison?" The troll climbs upon the other seat with some effort. They sit without a word for what seems to be several minutes, but most likely it is just a few seconds. Uncomfortable time passes much more slowly than normal time.

Hensley slowly begins the conversation but soon finds himself rattling question after question: "How does all this stuff fit into this tree? How did you show up at the old Moore barn? How did the nasty girls get the cooties? From where did you come? How did you know my name? Why haven't I seen you before? Are you really a troll? What's your name?" Hensley asks rapidly in one long breath.

"Why do you ask, Sir Hensley Addison? What is your reasoning? Shall I answer you as quickly as you asked?"

Hensley giggles and says, "Please answer as you would like."

"Shall I then not respond? Am I not from far away? Do not all of my things fit in my home quite nicely? Have you not seen me before in your dreams? Do not my stature and size, look and demeanor suggest that I am, yes, a troll? If you were to ask, would I not tell you indeed that my name is Gillo?"[35]

"Gillo! What kind of a name is Gillo?" asks Hensley childishly.

"Is not Gillo my kind of name?" asks the troll. "Would you not like to call me Gillo?" retorts the troll.

"Gillo it is," says Hensley.

"Shall I not then thank you, Master Hensley Addison?" The troll bows, standing in his chair.

---

[34] A pair of metal supports for wood burning in a fireplace.

[35] *Gillo* is a Latin word meaning "cistern," an underground reservoir for rainwater.

"Okay!" says Hensley. "Tell me what this is all about. Am I dreaming, or are you and all this real? Don't leave anything out. Tell me only the truth."

"Shall I not voice only what I know to be true?" answers Gillo. "Is it not so that trolls are found all around the world from Antarctica all the way up to the Arctic Circle? Are there not over two thousand known trolls worldwide? The greatest populations of trolls—are they not in Scandinavia, followed by North America and central Europe? Am I not uncertain about Africa, the Middle East, and northern Russia? Is it not highly probable that troll numbers worldwide could go as high as five thousand to six thousand? Should we not keep in mind, however, that trolls have never been numerous, even at the height of the trolls' golden age thousands of years ago? Is it not beyond doubt that troll numbers are in decline and have been for centuries? Does not the world now belong to humanity, and there seems to be little room left for trolls?"[36]

"What about you? Where did you come from? How long have you been in this tree?" asks Hensley with wide eyes.

"Is it not as the famed Captain John has told you? Is it not so? Does he not always speak only truth? Is he not a great man?" asks Gillo curiously. "Was I not traveling south on the Moon River when *Charity*, my river ship, was caught in the torrents? Was it not raised to the heights of a great tree? Did not the great captain find it and lower it to the riverbank? Did he not find my books, seed, and compass?"

"Wait a minute, wait a minute," interrupts Hensley. Hensley goes on, "First of all, why do you keep only asking questions? Even your answers are questions. Every time I ask you something, I feel like I'm the one who needs to answer. Can't you just answer without using what Mrs. Young taught us is an interrogative sentence? How about a single yes or no?"

---

[36] Statistic according to Trollwatch International.

Gillo responds, "Is not your question fair? Do you not ask rightly? Is it not true that I speak only in what you call the interrogative? How can I answer? How can I say the reason without the danger?"

"What danger?" interjects Hensley.

"Can you be patient with Gillo? Is it not true that if Gillo gives only the answer, that Gillo then is the one who knows? Is it not so that if Gillo knows, then he no longer needs to be? Do you not know that the day Gillo stops asking is the day that Gillo vanishes—evaporates?"

"Evaporates? What do you mean 'evaporates'?" asks Hensley.

"Shall I not be like the cloud that brought me? Did I not arrive with the rain? Shall I not then leave in a cloud?" counters Gillo.

"You're making my head spin," says Hensley. "Where did you come from, and where were you going? Have you been here ever since your boat got caught in the tree?" Hensley asks.

Gillo answers, "Did I not come from the far north wood, near the greatest of lakes? Did I not travel by way of creeks and streams, lakes and rivers? Has not my journey taken me to our destination? Have I not arrived these ninety and some years? Have I not come from there to here? Are your inquiries answered, my good Hensley Addison?"

Hensley continues his interrogation. "Have you been in Newburg, living in this tree, all these years? Are you alone? Do you have a family?"

Gillo laughs. "Do you not seek many studies of Gillo? Where shall I begin my speaking? Even though there are more than a few trolls, are we not solitary creatures like the hermit? Have I not lived here and there in Newburg town? Is not my home vast? Does not Gillo have family? Is not your family my family? Shall we not speak more another time? Should you not be leaving my tree home? Would we wish for our family not to worry? Should not Hensley inspect the bracket on Sue's swing? We would not want Hensley to fib, would we?"

Hensley says with concern, "Yes, I better get going. I think I've been gone a long time."

"Will you not remember to check Sue's swing?" says Gillo as he rises and begins walking to the staircase. "Shall we bid adieu, adieu?"

Hensley ascends the steps, which seem much steeper and longer than he remembered. He reaches the top, steps out into the fork of the tree, and closes the slate hatch. He hears the gruff voice: "Does Hensley remember to check the bracket—the bracket on Sue's swing?" Hensley looks over to the branch where the swing is attached and sees that the bracket that holds the swing is loose. He climbs down the ladder, goes to the barn for a wrench, and returns to tighten the bracket on Sue's swing.

While he is returning the ladder to the neighbor's fence, his mother, Mary, asks, "Hensley, what were you doing with the ladder in the tree?"

"Oh, nothing much, Mom. I was tightening the bracket on Sue's swing; it was a little loose," he answers with the biggest grin.

"Okay, dear. Be careful climbing the ladder, especially in that old tree; you never know what you might find up there," she replies.

"You bet, Mom; I'll be careful next time," Hensley answers, almost laughing out loud.

"Don't forget—church tomorrow," she calls.

"Okay, Mom. I'll be there in a minute," he answers.

———————

The teacher tells the children about David and the giant Goliath in Sunday school. During the discussion time, Hensley asks, "How tall was the giant?"

The teacher answers, "Some scholars say that Goliath was six cubits and a span tall, and that equals to be about nine feet and six inches."

"Wow, that's big!" the children reply.

Hensley raises his hand and asks, "If there were giants in the Bible, were there any dwarfs or trolls?"

"Well, Hensley, as a matter of fact, I believe it is in Leviticus … Let me see … Leviticus 21:20—yes, the Bible does mention dwarfs; however, it does not mention such creatures as trolls. Trolls are mythical fantasy characters only," replies the teacher.

"Could dwarfs be trolls?" Hensley asks.

"That all depends on what the definition of *troll* is. My goodness, Hensley, you have a lot of questions on our lesson this morning," answers the teacher with some amazement. The church bells chime the end of Sunday school class. As when all classes are dismissed, the children run as if from a fire.

The walk home from church is a bit windy and cold. It is too cold for ice cream but not too cold for apple pie à la mode after Sunday dinner. "Looking forward to dessert is as close a meaning of happiness as there is," half-jokingly bellows Great-Granddad with glee.

Sue pipes ups. "Like waiting for Christmas, Great-Granddaddy—like the night before Christmas."

"You've got it, kiddo,"[37] answers the captain laughingly.

---

[37] A loving term for little children.

# — Chapter 6 —
## Believing the Unbelievable

Love believes all things.
—1 Corinthians 13:7

ensley is between the proverbial rock and the hard place. He thinks, *What am I to do? I surely can't be sitting at dinner and say, "Hey, everybody, by the way, a troll lives in the old maple tree in our courtyard. I had tea and crumpets with him yesterday." Surely they would laugh and make fun of me. Well, maybe the captain wouldn't; he might believe me.*

*I can hear Grace: "Where did you have tea and crumpets, little brother?"*

*"I had them, thank you, in the large dining room next to the parlor in the hollow tree." That even sounds crazy to me. Maybe I should just keep it a secret. Maybe it was just a dream. What am I to do? What am I to say? How do I tell the untellable? Wait a minute—why do I need to tell anybody at all? What if I act as if Gillo is just an imaginary friend? Yeah, that's it; I will make him a make-believe friend.*

Sunday dinner is delicious, as always. The apple pie à la mode proves to bring lip-smacking happiness. Everyone has something to share. The captain tells a riverboat story. The doctor tells of the latest Arthur Conan Doyle's[38] *The Adventures of Sherlock Holmes* he is reading. He always ends these tales with a laugh and

---

[38] 1859–1930, Scottish physician and writer.

an "Elementary, my dear Watson—the game is afoot." Hensley, having read a few of the Sherlock Holmes short stories, loves to hear the doctor's renditions. With his thoughts on the troll in the tree, he too thinks, *Yes, the game is afoot.*

A few hours later, because it is a school night, the children are in bed by dark. Grace does get to stay up a bit later than Sue and Hensley, which, naturally, Sue doesn't think is a bit fair. Mary goes from room to room, saying prayers with her children, even Grace. She and Grace pray together in a more focused and grown-up way than she does with Sue and Hensley. When Mary prays with Sue, everyone likes to listen. Mary says a line, and Sue repeats it with childlike innocence. "Now I lay me down to sleep," Sue repeats.

Mary prays, "I pray the Lord my soul to keep." Sue again repeats. Mary continues, "If I should die before I wake."

Sue prays, "If you should die before you awake." Everyone gets a chuckle, for Sue is not willing to say, "If I should die before I wake." Then Sue says, "I'll pray, Mommy." And it begins: "God bless Mommy, Grammy, Great-Grammy, this and that …" The list will be endless if Mary does not interrupt with "Amen, my little princess. Amen."

Mary listens to Hensley say his prayers, and then they say the Lord's Prayer together. She then prays for him to be an upstanding young man, to do well in school, and to be honest and kind. She gives him a hug and a pleasant "Good night, my prince." Grandfather and Grammy Cora likewise make their good-night rounds.

Hensley falls fast asleep and steps right into a dream. He dreams again of the doors, except this time, he knows what and who is behind the green door in the maple tree. Instead of climbing a ladder to reach Gillo's tree home, he bends over and knocks on the door. Gillo opens the door and says, "Master Hensley Addison, will you not please come in?"

Hensley laughs and says, "You act as if I can fit through the door."

Gillo replies, "Can you fit through the door? Is it that you just cannot fit through this one door?" He then hands Hensley a key fob with a large brass key attached—at least, it appeared large in Gillo's four-fingered hand. The key is shaped like a pointing right hand. "Will not this key allow passage into my abode? Is there not a door in your dwelling that opens to mine?"

The next thing Hensley knows, he is back in his bed and realizes he has been asleep. "Was I dreaming? Am I dreaming?" Yet he finds in his hand the brass pointing-finger key. He looks at it closely; the key fob is engraved with the number seven. He utters to himself, "Flying catfish! The seventh door—it's the key to the seventh door." Hensley slips out of bead, dons his robe and slippers, steps out of his room, and turns to the left, and there it is—the seventh door. Was it, as he was told, placed there for architectural reasons or, as the captain said, "It just appeared one day"? The house is perfectly still and so quiet that he can hear the grandfather clock ticking from the dining room. His heart is beating like a drum. As he is reaching for the keyhole, the grandfather clock strikes midnight and scares the bejeebers out of him. He regains his composure, extends the key toward the never-opened door, slides the key into the hole, and turns it slowly to the left and then to the right, a full turn. There is a sucking sound like the breath of a chimney. With a poof of powdery dust, the door opens silently all by itself. "Hello?" he whispers. "Is anybody there?" He can tell that he is looking down a long corridor, but it is way too dark to pass. Even though the doctor has the newly invented flashlight, it is kept in the library. Hensley does, however, have a tallow candle and a box of safety matches in his room. He strikes the match and puts the flame to the candle, holds it out at arm's length, and slowly begins the walk down the long, dark corridor. Looking over his shoulder, he swallows hard, takes a deep breath, and proceeds. "This is unbelievable; the hallway is longer than the house is wide. How can that be?" he wonders. When he is several feet into his trek, the door closes behind him with a muffled swoosh. With a dry mouth and a thumping heart, the brave lad continues.[39] At the end of the hallway, there is another door, exactly like the door he left behind. It is locked. "Did I leave the key behind?" He searches his robe pockets. *There it is,* he thinks with relief. He imagines being locked in the hallway. Holding the candle with his left hand, he places the key in the second door and turns it clockwise one full turn. The door remains shut, but it is unlocked. He turns the knob and finds himself in another hallway. Yet this one has burning gas lamps lining the walls. It is a familiar setting; it looks like the troll's house. "It's Gillo's house," he murmurs. "Hello! Hello, Mr. Gillo—are you here?" he calls out just above a whisper. He continues walking and steps into what he remembers to be Gillo's parlor. "Hello, Mr. Gillo—are you home?" he cries a bit louder.

"Is that you, Hensley Addison? Is that you in Gillo's abode?" he hears Gillo call.

"I'm here. I'm in your parlor," Hensley answers. Gillo enters the room with his short, quick steps. Hensley giggles at the sight: Gillo has on a striped, oversized nightgown with a cap that hangs down almost to the floor and a pair of slippers that turn up at the toes, with fuzzy balls dangling at their ends.

Gillo, noting Hensley's outfit, lets out a little giggle himself. "Are we not a humorous sight?" states Gillo. "Which way have you been welcome to this humble abode? Did you use the pointing key for *syv-dør*?"[40] Gillo asks.

"The seventh door?" replies Hensley.

"You asked, and do I reply: *ja det er døren?*" Gillo answers with a wide smile.

---

[39] Author's note: I, like you, I have no idea what to expect; I'm stopping for a cup of tea.

[40] Norse for "door seven."

"What?" says Hensley, a bit befuddled.

"Did I not answer, 'Yes, that is the door,' in the tongue of my birth?" says Gillo.

## One Must Know Time and Place

For a thousand years in Your sight
Are like yesterday when it is past,
And like a watch in the night.
—Psalm 90:4

Gillo asks, "What is the time of the day, my dear Hensley Addison?"

Hensley answers, "The last I heard the clock chime, it was of the midnight hour."

"Are you not to worry of the hour? Is it not a new room with a new time?" Gillo states with a comforting assurance.

"What do you mean 'a new room with new time'?" asks Hensley.

"When you came in, did you not come from your time to mine, your realm to mine? Is not my home bigger than the tree it houses? Was not your last visit a long stay? Yet did you not notice how quickly it passed? Were you not gone from your realm a long measure of time? Yet was it not so that when you returned to your time and space, only a slight time had passed?" explains Gillo.

Hensley asks, "How can that be?"

Gillo pauses, thinks for a long while, rubs his wrinkled chin, and says, "Can Gillo explain time and eternity? May he attempt it? Does not the seventh door lead to a different room of time and space? Is not the Great Maker dwelling in today, yesterday, and tomorrow? Is He not here and there even now? Is it not called eternity? Time and space—are they not merely measurements? In your land, do we not measure time in years, days, hours, minutes, and seconds? Is not your space determined by length, breadth, and height? Are we not in just one room of reality?

In the heavens, is it not so that time even bends; small things may be great, and great things small? Are there not realms and times within realms and times? Are these not mere rooms? Is not Hensley Addison welcomed to Gillo's room?"

"Gillo," says Hensley, "I'm eight years old. How old are you?"

Gillo answers, "Am I not, in your time, 187 years of days?"

"Okay," says Hensley. "You've got me by 179 years. I'm not sure what you just told me other than, in this tree, size and time don't much matter. I think that might be all I need to know for now."

Gillo bows his head and smiles.

"Okay, I think I better be going. I've got school in the morning, and I have already been here for who knows how long," says Hensley.

"The way you came—should that not be the way you return to the realm of your house? Will you be full of care to not misplace the pointing key? And will you have not been gone but one minute of earth time? Will you not sleep well? Will I not now bid you adieu, adieu?" Gillo says, and he opens the door to the long hallway. "From now on, will I not always have a light in the corridor for you?" says Gillo.

"Good night, Gillo," says Hensley tiredly. Hensley walks through the hallway and opens and then locks the seventh door. He quietly slips into his room and into bed. He looks at the alarm clock on his nightstand; it reads 12:02 a.m. He then looks at the pointing key in his hand, smiles, and quickly falls asleep.

## The Key to the Seventh Door

Mrs. Young is teaching this morning about the Civil War, the Thirteenth Amendment to the Constitution, and the freeing of the salves by President Abraham Lincoln. Mrs. Young announces to the class, "We are honored this morning to have a special visitor with us who served in the Union Army during the Civil War; please help me welcome Major John Jaeger."

Hensley is surprised to see his great-granddad in his military uniform. As a matter of fact, he knows little about the captain's service during the war. He knows him as Captain because of his working on the stern-wheelers.[41] He had no idea that he was a major in the Civil War. There he is, nearly ninety-four years old, wearing his army uniform, and it still fits him as sure as if it were made for him yesterday. The blue of the uniform is not as deep as it once was. The shoulder cord is a bit frayed. Nevertheless, there he is, standing tall and proud.

"That's my great-granddad!" shouts Hensley as he runs up to him in front of the class. The captain gives him a hug and a pat and sends him back to his seat.

The major (captain) begins, "Mrs. Young and students, it is my honor to be with you this morning. I wish I could speak to you about better times in our country. But lest we forget and repeat the mistakes of our past, we must know and remember our history—the good as well as the bad. There is no greater tragedy than that of war. And there is no more sorrowful of wars than a civil war fought between good people over the rights of those created in the image of their Maker. In this terrible war, there were friends fighting against friends, and brothers against brothers. Our great nation was split, and its very survival was at stake. Thanks to Mr. Abraham Lincoln, the Union was preserved, and we are now a nation at peace with itself.

"What I would like to impart to you this morning is the role that our town, Newburg, had in this sad conflict. There was a great lady named Harriet Tubman; she was a runaway slave from Maryland who became known as the 'Moses of her people.' For over ten years, she risked her life leading hundreds of slaves

---

[41] A riverboat propelled by a paddle wheel positioned at the stern, or rear, of the boat.

to freedom along what became known as the Underground Railroad. It was a secret network of safe houses where runaway slaves could stay on their journey north to freedom. A few of those houses were right here in Newburg. The old Moore barn, young Hensley's house, known then as well as now as the Wilson Manor—and there were others; most are gone now."

"How did they get here? How did they get around without being seen?" ask the children.

"There have been many tales about that very thing," answers the major. "Some are tall tales at that. It has been said that there are tunnels all through Newburg. The stories have it that the freedom-seeking slaves would travel up the Moon River and that there would be a green lamp along the shores of the river where they could find safety. They say that there was a mighty oak tree next to the river that was hollow—washed away in the great flood of 1884—and that the slaves would enter the tree, and there were tunnels to different houses and places."

"How did they find the tree?" one student asks.

"Well, again, it's most likely more myth than history, but it is said that there was this little fellow who lived in that old tree and that he kept a little green lamp aflame and that it was he that guided the freedom seekers."

Without a thought, Hensley asks, "Was he a troll, Grandfather? Was he the Troll of Newburg?"

Mrs. Young says in a correcting voice, "Now, Hensley, this is a history lesson, not a fairy tale."

"Sorry, Mrs. Young," Hensley replies.

The captain smiles at Hensley and gives him a wink. Mrs. Young thanks Major Jaeger, and the class gives him an ovation, especially Hensley.

After school, Hensley runs home as fast as his feet will carry him. He runs right past his house to the carriage house, runs in the door, and, out of breath, declares, "Captain, Major, Granddaddy, how come you never told me about the war?"

"Easy, my boy—catch your breath. Have a glass of milk and some of Great-Gram's cookies—they're still warm," says the captain.

Hensley, without taking his eyes off of the captain, says, "Wow, thanks, Great-Gram—these cookies sure are good."

"Only one or two—you don't want to spoil your appetite," Gram answers.

Hensley, eating his cookies, declares, "Spoil my appetite! I think I'm making my appetite darned happy. Well, Granddaddy, how come you never told me about the war?" asks Hensley with a tone of downright disappointment.

"Hensley, my boy," begins the captain, "there are some things best forgotten. The memories of war are often some of those things. War is ugly. It is one thing to play soldier but another to actually be one in battle. If we old soldiers do talk about the war, we like to talk about the far-and-few-between good things."

"Like the safe houses and the freed Negroes?" says Hensley.

"Yes, my boy, like those good things. Now head on over to your house; I'll bet you have homework on the Thirteenth Amendment," says the captain with a smile.

"Thanks, Great-Gram, and thanks, Captain. I think I understand." Hensley waves good-bye and heads to his house.

## Imaginary Friends

Show me a child with imaginary friends
And I'll show you an adult with true friends.
—The Author

After homework, dinner, and family time, Hensley yawns and says, "Well, everybody, I think I'll hit the hay."

"So early?" Mary asks.

"Yeah, Mom, I'm tired and ready for some sleep and good dreams."

"Good night, Hensley," say all.

Off to bed heads Hensley. He actually is a bit tired and, sure enough, falls right to sleep and straight into a dream about the Underground Railroad, tunnels, and safe houses. As he did the previous night, he awakens as if he's slept all night. He looks at the clock, and it's not yet midnight. The house is quiet, and all are asleep. He is taken aback when he notices that the key to the seventh door is in his hand. "How'd that get here? I must have gotten it in my sleep." He sits up and thinks, *This must be a signal for me to visit Gillo.* He puts on his slippers and robe, steps into the hallway, and unlocks the seventh door. It opens as before, but this time, without the poof of powdery dust. Just as Gillo promised, the hallway is lit with gas lamps. The hall seems even longer than it did the other night. This night, he counts his steps—forty-nine. He taps on the next door, and straightaway, it opens. There stands Gillo, dressed in an unusual costume; he is wearing what looks like a military uniform with ribbons and medals attached to the jacket, and a small sword tethered to his right side.

"Good evening, Master Hensley Addison." He pronounces *Addison* as if it is two words; it somewhat sounds as if he is saying "Adam's son."

"Hey, Gillo. What's with the garb?" asks Hensley.

"Are you referring to my uniform? Is it not a day of honor for the brave who have served for good? Did not the great captain wear his uniform today?" replies Gillo.

"How'd you know about that? Did you know that Great-Granddad was a major in the Civil War?" says Hensley.

"Did I not serve with him in the tragic war? Was I not working for Mr. Lincoln in the Underground Railroad with the saintly Lady Harriet Tubman?" says Gillo, standing at attention and saluting.

"You were there. It was you in the hollow tree by the riverbank. You kept the green light for the slaves coming up the Moon River. You got them to the safe houses," says Hensley.

Gillo expounds, "From your revolution with Mr. Washington to your Civil War with Mr. Lincoln, was not Gillo nearby? Was not the year of Gillo's beginning 1723? Has not Gillo seen many beginnings of great men and notable events? Has not my duty been that of a soldier of the good and noble? Have I not been a guardian to the child that was destined for notable exploits? Have not all great men and women known what the elders call 'fairy tales' in their youth? Were they not called 'imaginary friends'? Will I not be considered your imaginary friend when revealed?"

Hensley, wide-eyed, responds, "What the heck? I know, don't say 'heck.' But what the heck? Are you actually as old as you say? You knew George Washington and Abraham Lincoln?"

Gillo interrupts, "Shall I not answer no, Master Hensley? Was it not so that I did not know them, but as children, they knew me? Was I not their friend, as I am now yours?"

"What are you saying, Gillo? I'm just a kid from Newburg. Are there others that know you in town? Are you friends with others?" asks Hensley.

Gillo bows and says, "Does not Master Hensley ask questions hard to answer? Shall I not try? Did not young John Jaeger know me as a friend? Did not the child Doctor Cola also know me as a friend? Did they not forget Gillo when they became grown? Was I not remembered only as an imaginary friend?"

Hensley asks doubtfully, "Gillo, are you a troll or just a small person? Were you born a troll? Are trolls just imaginary friends?"

Gillo answers with understanding, "Was I not born who and what I am? Are not others born with unlike colors of hair, eyes, and skin? Is it not true that all are born with certain ways of behaving? Are not those born of mankind born with a strong tendency to be kind and honest and yet others with a bent to lie and steal? Are not all creatures born with something received from earlier generations—all the way back to the first man and woman? Are not the qualities with which we were born good and just as some are hurtful and unfair? Is it not so that what matters is how we control both the good and the bad? Are we not able to learn how to increase the good and overcome the wicked? Do I not wish that I was greater in stature? Nevertheless, have I not learned to use my height as a gift? Is it not understood that the things I do are not magic? Are they not gifts that I have? Will you not grow from a baby to a young man, and someday you will be a full-grown man? Is it magic, or is it your gift of life? Am I not what you believe me to be?"

"I believe you to be a troll that lives in the maple tree in our yard," states Hensley.

"Then is that not who Gillo is—the troll that lives in your tree?" Gillo laughingly replies. "Would Master Hensley like some hot cocoa and shortbread? Due to my size, do you not think that I would not make good shortbread?"

Hensley is finding that Gillo has a sense of humor—dry humor but humor nevertheless. "I'd love some cocoa and troll bread," says Hensley with a laugh.

"Where would you like to have your cocoa and shortbread? Would you like it here in the parlor or the kitchen or maybe the dining room or the library?" Gillo asks politely.

"You have a library and kitchen?" asks Hensley, surprised.

"Do I not have rooms in my house like in yours? Do I not have these and more?" answers Gillo kindly.

"How many rooms are in this tree?" Hensley asks.

"Instead of counting in my head, may I show you through my home?" asks Gillo.

"A tour? Sure, I'd like that," replies Hensley.

"Have you not seen the parlor and dining room? Would you please follow me? Is this not the kitchen?" The kitchen is old-fashioned but well equipped and quite cozy. It has a wood-burning stove and a table ornately carved from a stump of a walnut tree, with chairs made from woven birch branches. There are hand-hewn cabinets with molded brass bird handles, and pots and pans hanging from a ceiling rack made of antlers. A gas chandelier hangs from the center of five rafters. The floor is made of gray slate. "Is this not the library?" says Gillo. It too is a fine room, with shelves of books from floor to ceiling. There are pictures of rabbits, fish, and strange-looking animals hanging between the shelves. There is also a portrait of Hensley's family.

"Who painted these pictures?" asks Hensley.

"Should not Gillo have learned to paint after 187 years?" he answers laughingly.

"It is a lovely house," says Hensley. "But where do you sleep? I didn't see a bedroom."

"Why would Gillo sleep, when all he needs is to rest?" Gillo answers.

"You don't sleep?" asks Hensley.

"Is not my rest better than your sleep? Do I not remain awake, but my body and mind rest well?" Gillo replies.

"Well, I sleep; I don't always want to, but when I'm tired, I can fall asleep anywhere. As a matter of fact, I'm kind of tired now. Maybe I should head back to my room realm," Hensley says with a yawn.

"Will you rest well, Master Hensley Addison?" says Gillo.

"I will, Gillo. You rest or do whatever you do well too," says Hensley as he heads toward the hallway.

As he is walking toward the seventh door, he hears, "Have I forgotten to say, adieu, adieu, my friend—adieu?"

Time goes on, and Hensley has several visits with Gillo, always at night after everyone is asleep. His visits are dreamlike. So it isn't that he is keeping things from his family; it is more like not sharing his dreams. Gillo often teaches Hensley about history, animals, insects, and trees, but mostly they speak of family, school, and Newburg. They often play games: checkers, pick-up sticks, and dominos.

Hensley and Grace continue to perform well in school. Fall ends, and winter arrives. During this time, Gillo is often missing, sometimes for days at a time or even a week or longer. He always tells Hensley of his need to be gone by simply saying, "Hensley Addison, has not Gillo been called to another room for a season? Will I not tell you when I return? Therefore, may I bid you adieu, adieu?"

# ⟾ Chapter 7 ⟾
## The Secret Is Out

No one ever keeps a secret so well as a child.
Victor Hugo, 1802–1885

t seems that almost every time Gillo is missing, an unusual amount of vandalism and thievery occurs in Newburg: trash is scattered about, the trash cans are crushed and ruined, streetlamps and windows in vacant houses are broken, and tools and toys and anything left out are missing and assumed stolen. Even Hensley's school and many churches are vandalized. The people in town are frightened by the hooligans or hoodlums causing such mischief.

"Sure sounds like the Newburg troll that ruined Mrs. Billingsley's white roses way back when," says the captain with regard to the shenanigans taking place in town. "Yes, sir, sure sounds like that old troll is up to his mischief once again. I wouldn't doubt it at all," he declares after dinner one night.

"Oh Dad!" says Grammy Cora. "You know that's just an old wives' tale. It's probably those Jonson and Brown boys; they've been caught doing mischief in the past. It's probably just those boys," she says.

"Yeah, Great-Granddad," says Hensley. "The troll wouldn't do such things."

Mary speaks in agreement with her mom. "Hensley, there's

no such thing as trolls. Captain, don't put that silliness into the children's heads."

Hensley sits silently in wonder. The captain mumbles, "Yup, must be that old troll."

That night, while in bed, Hensley lies with his hands behind his head, thinking about the destructive events that have taken place in Newburg. Each night that Gillo is not in his tree home, these terrible things happen. *Could Great-Granddaddy be right? Would Gillo do such a thing? What about the story about Mrs. Billingsley's roses? Don't trolls eat roses?* he wonders. Sleep doesn't come easily that night for Hensley. He tosses and turns, thinking about the possibility of his friend (his imaginary friend, some might say) being the cause of the vandalism in Newburg.

Restless sleep does finally come to Hensley's troubled mind. However, his dreams are as troubling as his thoughts. He dreams that noises from out back awaken him. In his dream, he gets out of bed, looks out his window, and sees trash being strewn all over the yard. He can't see who or what is throwing the trash; he can only see it flying through the air like frightened birds. Then he sees a red wagon full of tools and toys rolling around Paul and Mary's fence. He can't see who is pulling it, but he can hear a gruff, laughing voice singing, "Roses are white; flowers are true. I'm a nasty troll, so I bid you adieu, adieu."

Hensley awakens in a fearful sweat. His thoughts immediately turn to his friend Gillo. "I don't believe it. It can't be true. Gillo would never do such a thing and betray our friendship. I trusted him." He goes to wipe the perspiration from his brow and groans with an "Ouch!" He finds that he has scratched his forehead. Looking at his hand in the moonlight streaming through the window, he sees a shiny object hanging on his finger. It's the pointing key—the key to the seventh door.

Hensley jumps out of bed and throws on his robe and slippers, and with the key in hand, he quietly runs into the hallway and unlocks and opens the seventh door. The gas lamps are lit in the long hallway. Before he reaches the opposite door, it opens, and there stands Gillo with an enormous smile of welcome. "Do I not salute you with 'Buona sera, il mio amico,'[42] Hensley Addison?" says Gillo in his best gravelly Italian. "Is it not so very good to see you? Have I not been to Europe on troll business?" Noticing Hensley's expression of concern, Gillo asks, "What ails you, my young friend? Do I not perceive fear on your face? Will you not come sit a spell and inform Gillo of the cause of your pain?"

Hensley blurts out, "Are trolls thieves and vandals? Have you been about doing mischief, scattering trash, and breaking things? Did you eat Mrs. Billingsley's white roses ninety years ago?"

Gillo interrupts Hensley. "Will you not wait and take a breath? Will Master Hensley tell Gillo why he thinks such things? Here, will you not have some hot cocoa?"

Hensley calms down, takes a drink of the cocoa, and tells Gillo all that has been happening during his absence and about his dream. He adds, "Was it a dream? I am getting confused between what is real and my dreams. Am I dreaming now? Was I awake when the trash was being thrown about? Are you just in my mind? Are you what my mom calls my imaginary friend?"

"Is not my heart sad that my friend Hensley Addison would have to wonder if such things are true? Does not Gillo owe my friend a weighty apology? Am I not so very sorry that you have had to endure such thoughts? Am I not ashamed that I have exposed them to you? Was not Gillo sent to the continent of Europe by Mr. William Howard Taft?[43] Was I not there because of rumors of a coming Great War?[44] Is such knowledge necessary for eight-year-old Hensley Addison? Am I not innocent of local shenanigans?" Gillo says with a tear in his eye.

"The captain thinks it is you. He says, 'It's that old troll, the

---

[42] Italian: "Good evening, my friend."

[43] Twenty-seventh president of the United States, 1909–1913.

[44] World War One, known as the Great War.

Troll of Newburg.'" Hensley goes on, "My mom and the others think that trolls are old wives' tales."

## The Fallen Troll

Give light, and the darkness will disappear of itself.
—Erasmus[45]

"Is it not that villain Hubris?[46] Is it not that worker of darkness? Has not Hubris fallen from the good of light to the evil of darkness? Are you not safe in the light of day? Is not this evil agent only of the night? Has he not come but for the desire to take and destroy? Are not his ways crooked? Does he not lie when the truth would serve, even him, better?" Gillo sobs. "Must I not be on the alert? While I was absent, was he not present?" In great concern, Gillo speaks as if to himself. "When did he come? What is the evil that brought him? Was it just my protective absence or the wrongdoing of another?"

Hensley interrupts. "It was a troll then, but not you. Do you know this Hubris troll?"

Gillo answers, "Is it not so that none know him; they only know of him? Is it not fitting that trolls are solitary creatures, but Hubris is a separated creature? Was he not once in the room of the noble? Does not his mere name speak of the way he has tumbled?" Gillo turns and tells Hensley, "Shall it not be awhile until we meet in the evenings? Must I not be on the alert and watch the welfare of the city? Shall it not be that if you yield to my call of duty, this evil Hubris will flee?"

Hensley asks, "Should I tell my family that there are actually trolls? Should I at least tell them that you are not the one doing the damage?"

---

[45] Desiderius Erasmus, 1466–1536, was a Dutch scholar who used satires.

[46] In Greek tragedy: one with excessive pride toward or defiance of the gods.

Gillo, with concern, replies, "Shall we not wait to see the outcome of my dealings with Hubris? Would it not be good for Hensley to return to his room and wait to hear from Gillo? Shall we not wish each other good night, and shall I not wish you adieu, adieu?"

The next thing Hensley is aware of is the sun shining through his window, and he is waking up in his bed.

## A Slip of the Tongue

At breakfast, the doctor says, "Well, the good news this morning is that there was no vandalism last night. Constable[47] Henry and his volunteers found everything safe and sound."

"Thank goodness," says Mary.

Just then, Captain John walks in. "Good morning, all. Did they catch that troll last night?"

"Granddaddy!" says Mary in such a way that all eyes look at the captain with an expression of displeasure.

"I mean, did they catch those hooligan Jonson and Brown boys?" says the captain.

Grammy Cora pipes in with "Now, Dad, we don't know who is doing the mischief, so don't go blaming anyone until the wrongdoers are caught."

Hensley blurts out, "At least I know for sure that it wasn't Gillo."

Grace asks, "Who in the world is Gillo?"

"Yeah, Hensley, what's a Gillo?" says Sue. Everyone gives him a look that asks, *Who is this Gillo person?*

"It couldn't have been him. He was in Europe doing undercover work for President Taft. It was that evil Hubris. He's a dark troll," says Hensley with excitement. Everyone is motionless; they just sit there, looking at Hensley with their

---

[47] A peace officer with limited policing authority, typically in a small town.

mouths agape. Hensley, taking a bite of his oatmeal, looks up at all eyes pinned on him and says, "What?"

The captain slaps his knee and laughs. "I knew it was a troll. Yes sirree, Bob,[48] I said it was that troll all along."

"That will be enough of that," says Grammy Cora. "Hensley, who put that nonsense in your head?"

"Granddad, see what you've done?" shrieks Mary.

"What's a Gillo?" asks Sue.

"It's an imaginary character," Grace begins.

The doctor steps in with "Wait just a minute, everyone—wait just a minute. Let's all calm down now. The captain and I were talking with Hensley awhile back about the legend of a troll here in Newburg when the captain was just a lad. He, or we, meant no harm. It was just an old story the folks used to tell—my goodness, nearly a century ago. Nevertheless, boy, where in the dickens[49] did you come up with the names Gillo and Hubris? And who was in Europe for the president?"

Great-Gram has been standing at the door, listening to the entire goings-on, and says, "Just consider the boy's heritage; why wouldn't you expect him to have a wild imagination? John, you and those brothers of yours have told so many stories that the truth has been lost about ten deep. And you, Joseph—when you were little, you talked to rabbits. Now, that isn't so bad, but you insisted that the only reason you talked to rabbits was that they kept asking you questions—and you all wonder why Hensley has such an imagination. I'd be surprised if he didn't. Now, Grace and Hensley, you better be hurrying up; you're going to be late for school."

Great-Granddaddy hobbles out and whispers, "Yup, I knew it was that old troll."

---

[48] Earliest found use in 1846; considered to be a euphemism for "honest to God."

[49] *Dickens* is assumed to be a euphemism for the Devil.

# Dancing Lights

Not much more is said that day with regard to trolls. After school, Hensley goes into the courtyard alone and meanders over to the door in the maple tree. Sticking out of the side of the door is a small envelope; there is no writing on it, nor is there any writing on the paper inside. Yet scratched in the dirt next to the door are the words *invisible ink* and a scroll of a lemon peel. Hensley puts the envelope in his pocket, goes straight to the doctor's library, and asks his grandfather if he knows anything about invisible ink.

"Invisible ink, hmm … Let me think. Let's see—I have a book on writing materials. Let's take a look. Here it is—inks. India ink, natural ink, special inks … Yes, making invisible ink. 'The best ways of making invisible ink are using baking soda and water, writing with milk, and—the preferred method—making invisible ink with the juice of a lemon.'"

"How does it work, Grandfather?" Hensley asks.

"Let's see. It says, 'Get a plain white piece of paper and a small cotton swab. Dip the swab into the lemon juice, and write your message on the paper. After the juice dries, if you put the paper in direct sunlight or expose it to a lamp, the heat will cause the writing to darken to a pale brown so that your message can then be read.' There you go, my boy. Let me know if it works," says the doctor as he returns to what he is reading.

Hensley runs outside, but due to the clouds, there is little sun. So he goes into the barn, lights a kerosene lantern, and holds the paper next to it. The blank piece of paper warms from the heat of the lamp, and after several seconds, he sees a few faded brownish letters begin to appear: "Watch … for … the … aurora borealis[50] … It will be a sign that trolls are at war."

Hensley runs back into the doctor's library. "What does *aurora borealis* mean?"

---

[50] *Aurora* means "down," and *borealis* means "north wind."

"Well, my boy, that's the scientific name for what is known as the northern lights," he answers.

"What are northern lights?" Hensley asks with wonder.

The doctor thinks for a moment and answers, "Well, they are rather complicated, but for an easy answer, they are like giant curtains hanging and waving in the sky. They can spread from horizon to horizon and change from different soft greens to various blues. The earth is like a giant magnet. The sun sends out a solar wind made up of light particles that blow toward the earth. Why do you ask?" inquires the doctor.

As Hensley is running out of the library, he shouts back, "If there's going to be a troll fight, then there will be these here lights."

At dinner that evening, Hensley asks, "Mom, can I stay up a little later than normal?"

"Why, Son?" Mary asks.

"So I can watch for the Aurora's Boys."

"Watch for who?" she says.

The doctor, without looking up from his dinner, says, "Aurora borealis—he wants to watch for the northern lights."

"How do you know if there are going to be northern lights tonight?" asks Mary.

The doctor stops eating, looks at Hensley, and turns to Mary and says, "Let the boy watch."

Hensley goes out after dinner and looks north up the river a little after four o'clock. Five o'clock comes, followed by six and seven. At eight o'clock, Mary comes outside, along with everyone. "Well, Son, I'm sorry, but I guess there won't be any northern lights tonight."

All of a sudden, in the distant north, a greenish hue rises like a medieval dragon. The lights dance across the sky with the most beautiful array of colors and movement imaginable. Then they seem to gently sway like waltzing angels—back and forth, changing colors from amazing greens to the bluest blues and matchless purples. It is beyond a spectacular sight. All stand in awe, gazing into the night sky. Hensley watches in fearful awe. His eyes fill with tears as he prays for his fighting champion, Gillo. As quickly as the lights came, they are gone. "How did you know, Hensley? How did you know about the northern lights, Hensley?" asks Grace.

"Oh, just lucky, I guess," he says without thinking. The doctor and captain stay outside and talk for a while. Everyone else heads for baths and bed, chatting about the beauty of the aurora borealis.

While everyone is getting ready for the night, the doctor tells the captain about Hensley's questions, the invisible ink, and the aurora borealis. The captain says, "Listen, I know that some think me a bit old and senile, but I believe the boy. The stories told when I was his age about the Troll of Newburg were not a laughing matter back then, and just about the whole town believed it."

"So do I," says the doctor. "I believe the boy is telling the truth. I don't know if what he is saying is real or not, but I sure believe that he sees or knows something that no one else knows. What do you think we should do, Captain?"

"I think we should go to bed and pray that the good troll defeats the evil one. Good night, Joe," says the captain.

"Good night, Dad," says the doctor, giving his father-in-law an appreciative hug.

# ━➤ Chapter 8 ◆━
# When Trolls Battle

O Captain! My Captain! Our fearful trip is done.
—Walt Whitman, 1865

he beasts scurry in fear, dogs cower, and the trees shiver once trolls are at war. Never do equals in honor battle. Never does noble battle against noble. There are no worthy foes. The right must prevail. There are no rooms (realms) void of the battle against the evil forces of wickedness. Every realm of time must struggle against those who hate and reject the love of right. This night, there is a struggle for the myth of Newburg. The citizens are unaware of a great battle about to take place for their very peace and serenity. The northern lights have faded. The air is thick with fear. Not a creature is stirring. Only Hensley knows of the pending battle. The captain senses it by the experience of war.

The two trolls, though small in stature, require a sizable area to do battle. Being that they have the ability to move from realm to realm and space to space instantly, the contest can cover several miles. Trolls sense battle as birds sense a storm. There are three phases to the trollish art of war (called the Rules of the Three): the first is a battle of words, the second is a battle of wits, and the third and final is a battle of arms.

# The Battle of Words

The noble begin with a preemptive[51] strike of words. Thus, Gillo calls, "Hubris, is not your arrogance the cause of your fall? Are you not miserable in your way? Why have you attacked the good people of Newburg? Why not renounce your ways and turn to the good wherein you were created? Why not return to the dusk of the north, where you can have the liberty of the day? Would you not serve thy soul well to surrender and leave this realm? Do I not offer you grace and the way of peace? Shall not the battle end here?"

Hubris is silent for the longest time. Gillo hopes that he is weighing his offer of peace. After a deafening silence, Gillo calls again, "Oh, how I ask with hope that you are considering the noble offer?"

Hideous laughter breaks the silence. "You pathetic excuse for a troll, you sniveling tree dwelling rodent—I laugh that you dare challenge Hubris the Great. You cannot battle against me with your questioning words. You cannot even dare speak to me in sentences. All you can do is cower and fearfully ask me questions. I will not show you the least bit of respect to answer such trite words, you little warthog-faced buffoon. I do not fear the Maker, let alone a drone troll like you. You come to me with words because you cannot match my wit. I might even match wits with you with half my brain tied behind my back. Oh, what joy it would bring to crush you like the cockroach you are. Speak if you have the voice for it. I know you are cowering in your little boots."

Gillo answers, "Is it not so that those who are the weakest speak the loudest? Whom are you attempting to convince—me or thyself? Do you not understand that I do not hate you, but I must hate the things that you do? Do you not know that because you are my fellow troll, I am ordered to love you as myself? Yet

---

[51] Serving or intended to prevent an attack by disabling the enemy.

how can I love your evil ways? Must I not do all that I can to destroy them?"

Hubris shouts in greater anger, "I hate you and all that you stand for! I once was a question-asking coward like you. Then I decided I have knowledge; I have understanding. I am as good as anything and anyone. I can speak in my own self-goodness. If I question, it is only to mock. Come on, you twit; match my wits if you can."

## The Battle of Wits

"Is it not so that it shall be unfair for me to challenge you in a battle of wits, being that you most likely are unarmed?" mocks Hubris. "My kind helped outwit Samson to find that his strength was in his hair. We outwitted the Trojans with a wooden horse. Therefore, you cannot outwit me with your simple questions," continues Hubris.

"Shall we begin?" calls Gillo, and then he sets the rules for the match. "Shall not the first to stump the other choose the weapons for the battle of arms?"

"I doubt that you will get past the first round of my wits," taunts Hubris.

"Then why not go first?" says Gillo.

"I'll make the first very simple, just to make you feel good about yourself before I destroy you with my great intellect," scorns Hubris.

"Will you not give your riddle?" requests Gillo.

Hubris makes his first challenge. "I have two arms but no fingers. I have two feet, but I cannot run. I carry well, but I have found I carry best with my feet off the ground. What am I? Tell me if you can."

Gillo smiles. "Is that your riddle? Shall I not answer with ease? What is as good a labor-saving tool than a wheelbarrow?"

Hubris just groans and says, "I'm waiting!"

Gillo presents his challenge. "Does not mankind have a book of words called a dictionary? Is there a word in that book spelled incorrectly? If so, what is the word?"

Hubris wonders and says, "Being near perfect in knowledge and words, I would with ease find any misspelled words in any book."

Gillo says, "Are you stalling, dark troll?"

"Not at all," snarls Hubris. "The word spelled incorrectly can only be one: *incorrectly*. Mere child's play. Now I raise the bar. Answer this if you have my wisdom: Two humans have four daughters; each daughter has one brother. How many members are in this family?"

Gillo answers quickly, "Is it not so that there is only one brother plus the four sisters and the two parents? Does that not equal seven?"

Hubris screams in anger.

"Shall I not ask the next and, most likely, the final challenge of wits?" says Gillo calmly. "Is not there something greater than the Creator and more evil than the Devil? Something the rich need and the poor have? Something that if you eat it, it will kill you? What is it?"

Hubris begins to squirm. "That is a silly riddle. It is so stupid that I am sure it is without answer. If I do not agree with your answer to the riddle, then I will not yield to the game," shouts Hubris.

Gillo explains the riddle. "Shall I not give the answer? Is it not a simple one of morals? What is greater than the Creator, more evil than the Devil, needed by the rich, had by the poor, and, if eaten, will kill you? Is not the answer 'nothing'?"

Hubris curses and squeals, jumps up and down, and stomps his feet. "Name your weapons, and prepare to die," shrieks Hubris.

Page 83

# The Battle of Arms

"Choose your weapons, you sniveling dwarf. What will it be—swords, knives, lances, sticks and stones? Name your weapon," says Hubris through gritted teeth.

Gillo, in his gruff but forceful voice, states his choice of arms and the rules for the final battle: "Will not the battle be with hands?"

"Hands!" snarls Hubris. "Hands—I can destroy you with one blow of the smallest of my four fingers. I will choke you with my left hand. I will pound and pummel you with so many blows before you have time to say, 'Put 'em up.'"

Gillo smiles and says, "Will these not be the rules? Is this not the battle? Will we not each have a go until the match is decided? Shall we make the boundaries of the battle the area between the town and the heart of the river? Is this area not nearly one mile in width and two miles in length? Shall I not hide in this realm? Shall you not attempt to find and tag me? Will you not stand next to the stump of the old, hollow tree once used for the Underground Railroad? Shall you not count to ten and then begin to seek me? Shall it not be that if I can return to the stump before you find and tag me, then it will be my turn to seek and tag you? Shall it not be that the first to be duly tagged will be the loser? And shall not the loser of this battle leave Newburg, never to return? And shall he forever be banned to the great North, where the sun never rises?"

"What? You poor excuse for a troll. By all of my prideful and superior abilities, you wish for me to battle you, my arch enemy, with a game of tag. Tag! Tag?" screams Hubris. He puts on such a display of anger and bitterness that Gillo thinks that he might explode. He rants and rages for hours, screaming and cursing, banging his fat head against trees and rocks, kicking and shaking giant trees until branches fall to the ground.

Gillo stands and watches in humorous amazement. "Are you through with your tantrum?" Gillo asks.

Hubris curses and says, "I have agreed to the cursed Rules of the Three. Trolls cannot go back on their word in the contest of battle. I shall be tormented if I do not keep my word. You've made a fool of me. I will play your childish game to the utmost. I will defeat you, and then I will harass this town and that precious friend of yours, Hensley Addison, and his obnoxiously kind family. Know that you have brought my rage and revenge on those you care for most. Once I tag you and banish you to the great North, this town is mine."

"Shall not the battle begin? Must you not go to the stump and count ten?" instructs Gillo.

Hubris grumbles, places his head against the old stump, and begins his count: "One, you slime bug; two, you slug eater; three, you egghead; four, you warthog; five, you garbage guzzler; six, you dirt bird; seven, you mud ball; eight, you dumb bunny; nine, you pile of refuse; and ten, you putrid gnome. Ready or not, here I come to rid myself of you, you goody-two-shoes maggot."

With a whirl like a dust devil,[52] Hubris rushes about, screaming and howling insults toward Gillo. "I'll find you, you little twerp. I'll tag you to oblivion. You can't outrun, outthink, or outmaneuver me. I'm right behind you. I'm in a tree, now behind a rock. I can move faster than you can think."

As Hubris scurries about, Gillo moves from tree to tree. With each move, he stops and reveals himself to Hubris with "Am I not here; will you catch me if you can?" As soon as Hubris sees him, Gillo is in another tree or standing on a rock. Each time, Hubris curses and runs so quickly that he creates another dust devil. The hunt and chase and the hide-and-seek go on for hours. The two trolls move so quickly that a storm forms from the wind they create and the water that splashes up from the river. One second, Gillo is atop a tree, and the next he is riding a fish in the river. Hubris is within inches of Gillo. This time, Gillo is unaware of the nearness of Hubris.

---

[52] A small whirlwind over land, visible as a column of dust and debris.

Hubris lunges from a low branch of a tree and has Gillo in his sights. Gillo then twists and turns, runs like lightning, and touches the tree stump, shouting, "Am I not now olly, olly, oxen free?"[53]

Hubris once again screams and squawks insults and curses. "You cheater. You scoundrel. It is impossible for you to beat me," squeals Hubris.

"Is not the game now mine?" says Gillo. "Shall Hubris not hide and Gillo seek? Will I not soon begin to count ten?" Hubris scurries away with a flash, and Gillo begins his count. "Shall I begin with one and then two? Am I not now on three and also four? Are not five and six next to follow? Does not seven follow six, and is it true that eight comes after seven? Is not nine next to the last number in our contest? Now, last but not the least, is it not ten? Hubris, am I not coming to tag you and send you to the land of shadowy dusk?"

Unknown to Gillo, Hubris cheats and leaves the defined battleground. Hubris has a hidden supply of evil sorceries and wizardries. He returns to the battlefield with a burlap sack. He scurries as quickly as his troll legs will carry him to the river's edge. He shouts by throwing his voice to a distant tree, "Catch me if you can. I'll not move, because you're so dimwitted that I doubt that you will ever find me." Gillo works his best to find the illusive Hubris. He uses his ability to move and manipulate time. He knows that Hubris has found a cleaver hiding place—a place that most likely is not far from the tree stump.

Hubris has buried himself in the riverbank mud not far from the stump. He purposefully places the burlap sack next to his hiding place, so as to catch the attention of Gillo. It works. Gillo sees the bag and slowly inches up to the spot. He notices the fresh mud and clearly realizes that Hubris has buried himself in it. Unbeknown to Gillo, Hubris has a trained black mamba, the deadliest of snakes, in the burlap sack. Gillo sneaks slowly up to

---

[53] Originally "All ye, all ye, outs are free."

the spot where his arch enemy is hidden. He sticks his hand into the mud and says the game-ending phrase: "Is it not one, two, three on Hubris?" Before his hand reaches Hubris, the deadly black mamba strikes so quickly that it is able to bite Gillo ten times in an instant. Gillo gasps, and immediately the poison begins to squeeze his tiny lungs and heart. He stumbles back onto a pile of weeds and branches and falls motionless on the heap.

Hubris jumps from his pit and grabs his precious snake, kisses its venomous head, and puts it back in the burlap sack. With a hideous, demonic laugh, he sings and dances over the body of his rival, jumping with joy and waving his short arms in the air with a celebration of victory. He jumps up and down next to Gillo's body. A long branch lying under Gillo's right arm causes his lifeless arm to swing upward and tag the leg of Hubris. Hubris screams with great anguish, "Tagged! I'm tagged. Even in death, the scoundrel has defeated me." He lets out the most horrid of screams—screams so loud that every home in Newburg can hear the sound. Hensley is suddenly awakened with great dread; he knows something terrible has happened to his dear friend Gillo.

Hubris continues his raging, agonizing cries. "I'm banished. I'm banished—banished forever to the cold, desolate North. But you too, my enemy—you too. I may have been banished, but Newburg will have neither you nor me. Curse you. Curse you and this river town." Suddenly, the sky turns black; the wind fiercely howls and churns over the battleground, and with a violent gust, Hubris is hurled away, tumbling and screaming.

## Gillo's Sacrifice

Several days pass. Newburg is quiet. There are no more cases of vandalism or things being stolen. However, the quiet is an eerie silence. There is something amiss, but nothing that can be explained. Birds are not singing. Dogs and cats just lie around listlessly. Even the river has an appearance of being troubled. Again, these things are not something explainable; they just are.

Grace and Hensley go to school as usual. Sue plays, and adults do what adults do. Things are normal in the Wilson house, but as in the rest of the town, there is something just not right. Nothing more has been said about trolls. However, Gillo has not left Hensley's mind. There is a dark shadow over his young life. He can't shake it, nor does he wish to until Gillo returns.

The body of Gillo lies where he has fallen. The wind that carried Hubris away has covered the body with several inches of leaves and brush.

One evening, when all are in bed, Hensley searches for the key to the seventh door but cannot find it. He tries the door, but it is locked as tightly as ever. He lies in bed, tossing and turning, doing his best to fall asleep so that hopefully he will dream and waken to the return of Gillo. After what seems like hours, he is asleep. His dreams come. In his dream, he is awakened by the sound of his name: "Hensley, Hensley. Hensley Addison, are you not my friend?" The call is the gruff voice of Gillo. It says sorrowfully, "Am I not lost, never to be found? Am I not hopelessly gone? Has not my foe defeated me by treachery? Do you not have the key? If there is any hope for my return from this realm—do you not have the key?"

"What key? Is it the pointing key to the seventh door?"

The gruff voice answers, "Are there not three doors?" And Hensley hears, "Am I not gone, gone, gone?"

Hensley is awakened by the wind whistling through the trees outside his window. The whistle makes the same gruff sound. Hensley is at the point of not being able to tell dreams from reality. "Was I dreaming? Did Gillo call, or was it just the wind in the trees?" Tossing and turning, he returns to sleep.

The following morning is a Friday. Due to a teachers' conference, there is no school, leaving the children a long weekend. Hensley is up at the crack of dawn (due to the approaching winter solstice,[54] dawn comes later and the sunset earlier). The family has breakfast together. Sue calls it a "Yahoo breakfast" because Hensley and Grace are home instead of at school. Sue loves her brother and sissy. When they're home from school, she follows them around like a little shadow.

Hensley and his shadow, Sue, head out to the pavilion, where the captain and the doctor are sitting by a glowing fire. "Great-Granddad, Grandfather, can I talk to you?" Hensley asks. Sue sits on the captain's lap up close to the fire. It is a bit chilly.

"What is it, my boy?" asks the captain.

Hensley begins, "You know the other day when we were talking about all the shenanigans taking place in Newburg? And how you, Great-Granddad, said you thought it was the old Troll of Newburg? And I said Gillo wouldn't do such a thing. Well, I visited him that night, and he told me that it wasn't him but another troll named Hubris. Hubris is an evil troll, and it was him doing the vandalizing. The other night, there was the aurora borealis, the northern lights. The northern lights indicate that trolls are about to go to war. Gillo told me that he was going to battle Hubris. Do you remember the horrible screaming and wailing we heard the other night, which was so awful and loud that the whole town heard it? It must have been the battle between Gillo and Hubris."

"Slow down, son—slow down," says the doctor.

"Yeah, slow down, Hensley," says Sue.

The captain just laughs and says, "Go on, boy."

Hensley continues his story. "Last night, I had a dream that Gillo was calling me to help him. I just know that something is terribly wrong. He kept saying that he was gone but that I had the key to get him back. I said, 'What key?' and he said, "Are there not three doors?' I've been through two of the three doors; the little green door in the tree is Gillo's door."

---

[54] Marks the onset of winter, the time of the shortest day, about December 22.

Sue says, "Hensley, can you fit through the little door?" Both the captain and the doctor look at Hensley for the answer.

"No, Sue, I can't fit through the door, but there is a hatch in the tree that is big enough. Plus, when I visit Gillo, I use the seventh door upstairs."

The doctor interrupts with "Hensley, you have a fantastic imagination. That is an incredible story, but I'm afraid it is just a story."

"I believe you," says Sue.

"Me too," says the captain. "I've always known that the troll was real. Yes, sir, I've always known the story was true. What do you want to do, my boy? How can we help?" says the captain.

The doctor just stares at the captain in disbelief. "Listen, Hensley—and you too, Captain—it is just something you are imagining; it is not real."

The captain, speaking more to the doctor than to Hensley, says, "His imagination is evidence to the reality of the troll's presence."

"What?" says the doctor in disbelief.

"Let's see what he wants, give him a chance, and see what comes of it," says the captain with a confident grin. "Come on, Joe—think about when you were young. Don't you remember those things that the adults called imaginary? Now that I'm old, I think that the joys of my youthful imagination have returned. Let's have a go at helping Hensley. What can it hurt?" lectures the captain.

"I'm not sure, but I think the key that Gillo was talking about is the key to the wardrobe," says Hensley. "I've opened the other two doors. The wardrobe is the only door left."

"Okay, okay!" says the doctor. "Let's go take a look inside the wardrobe."

"Can I come too?" asks Sue.

"Sure, kiddo—come on," says the doctor.

# The Key to the Wardrobe

"There it is," says the doctor. "Come on, Sue; get on my shoulders. On top of the wardrobe, you'll find an old key. Reach around; you'll find it."

"Got it, Grandfather; I've got it," Sue says.

"Attagirl. Let me see ... I've not opened this thing forever." With a click, the door unlocks, and the doctor pulls it open. "I know it's in here somewhere. Yes, here it is." The doctor pulls out a dusty old cigar box.

"That's it—a little cigar box?" exclaims Hensley.

"I haven't seen that box in a coon's age,"[55] says the captain. "I gave you that box—what is it—nearly sixty years ago?"

"I was about Hensley's age when you gave it to me for safekeeping. I've been its guardian ever since," replies the doctor.

"Open it up, Grandfather—open it up," says Sue with great excitement. The box is tied with a piece of twine. The doctor opens the cigar box, and all eyes are over his shoulder, straining to see what's in it. They all sit on the sofa as the doctor takes each item out of the box as if it is a precious treasure. The first is a small brass compass with an adjustable sundial. The second item is a bundle of two books tied together with ribbon. The third and final item is a small, soft fur bag. "What do you think these things mean, Hensley?" asks the captain.

"I don't know," he answers.

"Let's see if we can figure it out," says the doctor. "You got me up here, so I might as well play detective and use my powers of deduction like Mr. Sherlock Holmes." Everyone chuckles, including Sue, even though she has no idea what her grandfather is talking about. "Let's start with the compass. What are compasses used for?" he asks.

Page 91

[55] The expression dates to the early 1800s and to the folklore belief that raccoons live long lives.

Hensley says, "To find your way."

"That's right, Hensley. What about the books?" the doctor asks.

"How can we know if we can't read them?" Hensley answers.

"I agree," says the doctor, and the captain and Sue concur. "Lastly, there are these very tiny seeds. I have no idea what species of seeds these can be," says the doctor. "So let's go with what we do know. We know that a compass is for finding one's direction."

## The Compass

"What direction does a compass point, Hensley?" asks the doctor.

"It points north, Grandfather."

"That's right. Wait a minute—Captain, which way is north?"

"Up the river, Joe; you know that."

"Look here," says the doctor. "Which way is this compass pointing?" Everyone looks at it at the same time.

"It's pointing north. No. Now it's pointing west. Look, now north again, and now it's pointing west," says Hensley. "It's like the compass is trying to tell us something. Can we follow it, Grandfather? Can we?"

"I'm game," says the captain.

"Me too," yells Sue.

"Well, it's a nice day for a walk, and we sure can't go that far. The river is less than a half mile away," says the doctor.

Like crusaders on a mission, they walk down the steps, out the front door, across Luna-Vista, and over the hill, toward the river. When they reach the river, the doctor says, "Now what?"

Hensley shouts, "Grandfather, look! Look at the compass." It is spinning like a top and then stopping, spinning, and stopping. Each time it stops, it points south, down the river. "Can we follow it, Grandfather? Can we?" pleads Hensley.

"You bet. I've never seen anything like this," says the doctor.

"I've been on this river my whole life and followed compasses, and neither have I," says the captain. The further they walk, the more unusual the compass acts. The needle starts to squirm and jiggle. "Keep going," says the captain. All of a sudden, the needle starts spinning faster and faster until it breaks and falls to the bottom of the brass case.

"Now what, Grandfather?" asks Hensley with hope in his voice.

"I don't know, my boy; I don't know," says the doctor.

Sue bends down and picks up a shiny object. "Look here. Look what I found," Sue says, holding a muddy but bright tiny object.

"Let me see that," says the captain, taking it from Sue and wiping it on his trousers. "It's a sword," he says with a bit of astonishment.

"It's Gillo's sword," shouts Hensley with sheer excitement. The captain and doctor are speechless.

"It is a small sword," says the doctor, a bit bewildered.

"He's here; I know he's here. We've got to find him. Please, Captain. Please, Grandfather. Please. I know he's here," pleads Hensley.

"Okay, son. We can look, but we can't stay too long. It will be dark before we know it," says the doctor. "Sue, you stay put right here. Captain, you look upriver. Hensley, you look around here, and I'll walk downriver a bit. If anyone finds anything, just give a holler," orders the doctor.

They all do their best looking, not knowing what they will do if they find anything, especially a troll. Sue does what four-year-old children do when next to water; they throw things to make a splash. Sue throws rocks and twigs and just about anything she can pick up. As she is standing on a small mound of dirt and branches, she slips and almost falls into the river. Being all muddy, she begins to cry, worried that she might be in trouble. Hearing her cry, everyone comes running.

"You okay, sweetie?" asks the captain, brushing the mud off of her dress.

"We better be going. It's growing late, and Sue is likely to be getting cold," says the doctor.

"If you wish, Hensley, we can come back tomorrow and look some more," says the captain with compassion for Hensley.

"My shoe!" cries Sue. "I lost my shoe; it must be stuck in the mud." She runs back to where she fell. "I got it," she shouts. Then, with a start, she screams, "Look! Look! There is a dolly under the branches. Get it for me, Hensley. Please."

Hensley brushes aside the twigs and branches, and sure enough, there is a worn-out, mud-covered baby doll. All of a sudden, Hensley cries, "Wait! Wait! It, it, it's Gillo. Grandfather, Captain, hurry." The captain and doctor come running. They bend down, and sure enough, they see a small, lifeless body. "It's Gillo. Please help him, Doctor—please help. Do something."

The doctor puts his ear to the troll's chest, feels for a pulse, and looks into his eyes. With sadness in his voice, he says, "I'm sorry. I'm so sorry, Hensley. I don't think there is anything I can do."

Hensley weeps bitterly.

## The Little Books

The doctor covers the miniature body with his coat, gently lifts it in his arms, and begins to carry the lifeless troll up the hill.

"What are we going to do with it?" asks the captain.

"I don't know. I'm thinking; I'm thinking," says the doctor. Now Sue is crying because her brother is crying so sorrowfully. The captain is doing his best to calm the saddened children and himself.

"Hensley!" yells the doctor. "Run ahead, get the little books from the wardrobe, and bring them out back to the barn. Don't tell anyone what you are doing—hurry!" The doctor asks the captain, "Dad, will you take Sue in and explain to the ladies what is going on? Ask them to please stay in the house and not say anything to anyone. Bring Sue's doll cot to the barn. Let's see what we can do."

Hensley, the captain, and the doctor arrive at the barn at the same time. The doctor lays the lifeless body of the troll in the doll bed and covers him with the small blanket that was in it. Hensley brings the books.

"Dad, strike a couple of the lamps, and bring them closer to the workbench. Hensley, hand me those books. Thanks, Dad. What do you make of these writings? They look like hieroglyphics.[56] Hensley, you've been with this troll—"

Hensley interrupts, still teary-eyed. "Grandfather, his name is Gillo."

The doctor responds, "I'm sorry, Hensley. You've been with Gillo—what do you think these writings or figures are?"

Hensley looks at them and says, "I've seen marks like them on the furniture and picture frames in Gillo's tree. I think that they are just designs. They were on the envelope he gave me with the invisible-ink message."

Everyone stands there, wondering, *Is there anything that can be done. Is Gillo dead?* The doctor's eyes open wide, and he yells, "Invisible ink! Hand me a lantern." He takes the lantern and holds it next to the miniature book. As he does, letters begin to appear between the characters.

## The Seeds

The doctor continues, "Look—words are appearing more clearly. *'Accipere semina … misce cum terra et aqua … potus.'* It's Latin. I hope I can remember my Latin from my chemistry days. It says, 'Take seeds … mix … with earth and water—drink.' There's

---

[56] Incomprehensible symbols or writing.

more: '*Vigilant ad venenum semina.*' That translates to 'Be wary of the poison seeds.' How many packs of seeds are there?"

Hensley looks in the sack. "Three—there are three vials of seeds. Which ones are the good ones? How do we know that these will cure Gillo? What are you going to do, Grandfather?"

"Hand me the other book." The doctor takes the second book and holds it to the flame. Words likewise begin to appear. "'*Spes Mus fortis sit … fidem necessario esse fortiori.*' This is more difficult; these are not scientific words. I'm not sure, but I think it says, 'It takes true hope … and real believing.' Hensley, go to the kitchen and get Grammy Cora's pestle and mortar."[57] While Hensley is gone, the doctor tells the captain, "I'm not sure, but all the signs show that Gillo is dead. He could, however, be in some suspended state. This might sound crazy, but it is like he is mainly dead but maybe not totally dead. However, if we give him the wrong seeds, he will be completely dead."

The captain thinks for a minute and gives his wisdom. "It has to be up to Hensley. If it takes, like you read in the book, 'true hope and real believing,' there will not be another person on earth that will match his hope and belief."

Hensley comes running with the pestle and mortar. The doctor looks into Hensley's eyes and says, "Son, no one has more hope and believes in Gillo more than you. Bring me a bit of soil from the garden, and fetch a cup of water from the well."

Hensley quickly returns with both. He hands the soil and water to the doctor. "Now, Hensley, hand me a vial of seeds from the fur sack."

"Which one, Grandfather?" Hensley asks with concern.

"You must choose, son. It has to be your call. It is your hope and your belief that will choose the right pack of seeds."

"Only believe, Hensley—only believe," the captain says with tender confidence.

---

[57] A tool used to crush, grind, and mix solid substances.

Hensley takes the three vials out of the sack. He looks at them closely. "This one, Grandfather. Take this one."

The doctor takes the vial, breaks it into the mortar with the earth, and grinds them together with the pestle. "Hensley, pour in the water slowly." As he does, the doctor grinds the mixture until it's a syrupy amalgam.[58] The doctor pours the mixture into the glass that held the water and hands it to Hensley. "Dad, help me hold up Gillo. Hensley, slowly—very slowly—pour the liquid into Gillo's mouth."

## The Wait

Patience is bitter, but its fruit is sweet.
—Aristotle

"Why isn't anything happening?" asks Hensley anxiously.

Lying Gillo down, the doctor answers, "Son, this isn't a fairy tale where everything always works or where everyone lives happily ever after. This is real life, and in real life, things do not always work out exactly how we would like. This isn't magic. We are giving Gillo, hopefully, medicine that will cause him to be restored to health. We have done all that we know to do. Now it is time to rely on true hope and real belief. So all we can do is hope and pray."

"And believe, right, Grandfather?" says Hensley.

"Yes, and believe," the doctor answers, looking toward the captain with despair.

"What are we going to do now?" asks Hensley.

"We're going to wait," answers the doctor.

"I'll stay here in the barn with Gillo," says the captain. "Tell Great-Gram just to bring my dinner here. I'll be fine; I've got the potbelly stove and a few lumps of coal. Gillo and I will be just fine

---

[58] A mixture or blend.

here in the barn. You all go into the house and have dinner and get a good night's sleep. If anything happens, I'll give a whistle; you'll surely hear my whistle."

"No!" says Hensley. "I'm not leaving."

"Oh yes you are, my boy. You'll do neither Gillo nor yourself any good being tired. Now skedaddle,"[59] orders the captain.

"Come on, son—let's go. I'm sure dinner is on the table, and everyone will be waiting," says the doctor.

Sometimes, but not often, it's okay to mope.[60] For Hensley, this is one of those times. He's worried, confused, and experiencing something few eight-year-old boys experience: the loss of a friend that is a troll.

Everyone is already quietly seated for dinner. Hensley and the doctor stop at the kitchen sink and wash their hands (usually not an acceptable thing for them to do). The doctor sits down and grabs Grace's hand, she grabs the next hand, and so on until all are holding hands around the table. "Tonight, I think it would be good for Hensley to pray," says the doctor. Everyone bows his or her head.

It is quiet for what seems to be the longest time. Then, with stuttering breath, Hensley begins to pray. He gets out one phrase—"Dear Lord"—and then breaks down in tears.

"It's okay, Son; it's okay," comforts Mary, also in tears for her son.

"Take your time," says Grammy Cora. "We're in no hurry."

He begins again. "Dear Lord, my friend is very sick. I'm not even sure if he's not already with You in heaven. Please let the seed medicine work. Please wake him up. He's watched over Newburg and Great-Granddad and Grandfather when they were boys like me, and now he has been watching over me and our family. I sure want Grace, Sue, and everyone to get to know him like I do. Bless our food, and bless us one and all."

Page 98

---

[59] Depart quickly or hurriedly.

[60] To be unhappy, gloomy, sad.

And everybody says, "Amen." The food is served, but not much is eaten.

Grace speaks up first. "Hensley, I'm so sorry that I didn't believe you. It will never happen again."

Then Mary speaks. "Son, it's not that we didn't believe you; it was that we didn't believe that Gillo was real. We believed that he was just your imaginary friend."

"When Gillo is better, can I play with him?" asks Sue.

Hensley, for the first time, smiles and says, "I'm sure Gillo would be honored to play with you, as long as you don't put a dress on him." Everyone laughs.

Dinner ends, and the cleanup is almost silent. Hensley asks, "Mom, can I go out to the barn for a little while?"

Mary looks at her dad, and he gives a nod. "Sure, Son, but just for a minute. Great-Granddad will let us know if there is any change."

Hensley, without a word, heads to the barn. He walks in not knowing what to expect or say. Great-Granddad says with compassion and hope in his voice, "Nothing yet, my boy— nothing yet."

Hensley walks over to the cot. He just stands there for a few seconds and talks to Gillo. "Gillo, I don't know if you can hear me, but if you can, please wake up. You need to tell us about the battle. I'll bet you gave that Hubris a good licking. It's getting close to Christmastime. You waking up would be the best present ever." He turns to the captain. "You'll be sure to whistle real loud if he wakes up, won't you, Great-Granddad?"

"I'll make the house shake I'll whistle so loud. Now go get some rest. I'm going to put my feet up close to the stove and keep both eyes on Gillo."

Hensley walks back to the house. On the way, he stops by the little green door in the maple tree, stares at it for a few seconds, and goes into the house.

Everyone gets ready for bed; they say their good nights and

prayers. Tonight, everyone prays hard for Gillo. Mary, Grammy Cora, and Grace pray especially for Hensley. Sleep doesn't come easily to anyone but Sue. Little children have an innocent trust. Too bad it's not something that can be kept as we grow older.

Exhausted, Hensley prays himself to sleep. There are no dreams this evening or whistle from the barn. He awakens with the first sounds of morning.

## Chapter 9

# The Surprise of Joy

Weeping may endure for a night,
But joy comes in the morning.
—Psalm 30:5

he next morning, everyone stirs early. All are
descending the stairs at the same time, when all of
a sudden, there's a loud *"Pheweeee."* Everyone looks
at each other and runs the rest of the way down the
stairs and through the hallway and dining room; some run out
the mudroom, and others run through the kitchen. No one runs
as fast as Hensley. As he runs into the barn, he sees the captain
standing over the cot in his bare feet. His eyes are as big as saucers.
"I never closed my eyes, but he's not here. He's gone. There's
nothing here but this blank piece of paper pinned to the cot."

"Get the lamp, Hensley," cries the doctor. Hensley grabs the
lamp and quickly holds the paper to it. "Here it comes. Here
come the letters: 'Is it not a very good new day? Does it not
remain true that Gillo cannot be in the daylight? Even though
he slept not, did I not slip away without the great captain seeing?
Hensley, my friend, if they would honor Gillo, will you invite the
family to my abode at twilight? Do I not have much to say and
much cause to be thankful? Until then, may I say adieu, adieu?'"

Hensley starts jumping up and down with the biggest smile

ever. Everyone is clapping and smiling and hugging Hensley. "Yahoo! Yahoo! Yahoo!" he shouts.

The captain simply says, "It was Hensley's true hope and real believing."

Sue asks, "Can I play with Gillo now?"

"Soon, little sister—soon," answers Hensley with a hug.

Grammy Cora says, "I think this calls for a good breakfast. I think we're going to a party tonight."

## A Party

Going so soon? I wouldn't hear of it. Why,
my little party's just beginning.
—L. Frank Baum, *The Wonderful Wizard of Oz*, 1901

The day is festive, with much laughter and lots of smiles. Even the birds seem to know that something good has happened. It is a terrific day. Grammy Cora says, "What shall I bring? Should I bake a pie?"

The doctor says, "We should bring a gift; how about a good book?"

Grace says, "What shall I wear?"

Sue says, "How do we get in the little door?"

Hensley smiles and answers everyone's concerns: "Grammy, whatever you bring will be great. But the favorite things trolls like to eat are flowers—roses in particular and white roses best. Grandfather, a book would be nice. Grace, I've always worn my pajamas." He then asks, "What time is dusk?"

The doctor says, "I've looked in the *Farmers' Almanac*, and it says that there is a new moon and that the sun will set at five forty. We should give it a few minutes and go nearer six."

Sue asks again, "So how do we get through the little door?"

"We don't," says Hensley. "We go through the seventh door upstairs."

It is a funny sight to see everybody's mouth drop open at the same time. "I didn't think about where Gillo lived and how we would get there," says the doctor.

Hensley then says with a giggle, "Let me explain—no, better yet, let me show you when it's time. Seeing is better than explaining." Then he thinks to himself, *The key—the pointing-finger key—where is it?* He runs to his room and looks around frantically—no key. He thinks hard, steps out into the hallway, and glances over at the seventh door. There, in the keyhole, is the key with the number-seven key fob hanging on its chain. He removes it and puts it in his pocket with a smile. By five thirty, everyone is in the dining room, staring at the grandfather clock. The captain and Great-Gram arrive dressed to the nines.[61] Great-Granddad and the doctor sit drumming their fingers on the table. Mary has her legs crossed and is nervously shaking her foot. The ticking of the clock seems to be slower than normal. With butterflies in their stomachs, they wait.

The clock chimes the "Westminster Quarters"[62] and strikes six times. Hensley leads the way, followed closely by Sue. Usually the adults lead, but this evening, the order is from the youngest to the oldest. No one says a word, except Sue; she's singing all the way.

Hensley unlocks the seventh door with the odd-shaped key. (Now imagine there being a door in your house that has never been unlocked and seeing it opened for the first time.) As before, the door opens without a push. Hensley begins walking down the long, well-lit gas-lamp hallway. After he takes a few steps, he looks over his shoulder and sees everyone still just standing at the door with an expression of uncertainty.

"Come on—we're going to be late," says Hensley.

Grammy Cora is holding on to the doctor's arm, and

---

[61] Fashionably dressed—nine being the highest single-digit number.

[62] The name for the melody chimed by the clock bells.

Great-Gram and the captain are holding hands. Grace is trying to catch Sue's hand, but Sue is dancing and twirling. The captain says in great wonder, "How in the world can this be?"

Hensley answers, "We're no longer in that world." Within a couple of feet of the end of the hallway, the next door opens, and there stands Gillo, dressed in as fine of clothes as anyone has ever seen. He looks like a royal. He is wearing a red silken coat with gold buttons and shoulder ribbons. Tied at the waist is a wide velvet belt. He is wearing white leggings and golden slippers turned up at the toes. He places his right hand over his midsection, lifts his left arm to the side, and bows his head nearly to the floor, saying, "Am I not so highly honored to have you as guests in my home? Are you not welcomed? Will you not come in?" As they enter, they do so quietly. The men give polite nods of the head, and the women curtsy. "Will you not please come and have a seat? Is not dinner waiting?" says Gillo.

The table is elegantly dressed with Venetian glass, the finest gold-rimmed china, and shimmering silver-and-gold cutlery. In the center of the table is a beautiful vase with a dozen perfectly formed white roses. Each setting has an embroidered name tag. The captain is seated at one end of the table, and the doctor sits at the other. Next to the captain is Great-Gram. Next to the doctor are Grammy Cora and Mary. Grace and Sue are on one side of the table, and Hensley and Gillo are on the other. Everyone is still and quiet, as if at a royal banquet with the queen of England. Gillo taps his glass and says, "May I propose a toast?" He holds his glass in the air as he stands on an ornate box placed on his chair. Everyone raises his or her glass, looking toward Gillo. "Shall I not raise my glass in honor of those that I have been honored to safeguard? Am I not now toasting them for safeguarding me? Shall we not drink to the love of life and good days?" He nods, raises his glass a bit higher, and sips a drink, as do all.

"Yummy!" shouts Sue. "That is delicious."

"Yes, it is," says Grace. "What is it? It is wonderful."

"Is it not the nectar of the sweetest of vines and the tenderest of berries?"

The captain says, "I too would like to make a toast. I salute Hensley Addison for his hope and belief when there seemed to be no hope, and I salute Gillo, who is a friend to every child with the imagination to believe. Cheers." All drink.

Gillo asks Grace to serve. The dinner consists of a clear-broth mint soup with truffles, tender roots and gourds, and a berry-and-greens salad. Some courses are served hot, and others are fresh and cold. For dessert, they have hot cocoa and a fluffy wafer made from coriander seed. All is most delicious.

After dinner, Gillo gives all a tour of his tree home. They then go into the parlor, where there is a glowing fire in the hearth. Gillo stands in front of the fireplace, thanking everyone again for coming. He says, "Do you not have many questions? Are not questions better than statements? Before you ask, shall I not do my best to explain?" He then gives an account of who he is; his age of 187; how he came to Newburg; the little boat, *Charity*, that the captain found as a boy; his work with presidents; and the help he gave Harriet Tubman with the Underground Railroad and the safe houses. He speaks for nearly an hour, and not a soul is bored. He is most amusing, and his gruff voice and gestures are entertaining.

He speaks with the biggest grin; one cannot but help to likewise smile. He says even the more grievous things with a peaceful joy. When asked about the great battle with Hubris, he explains in detail the Rules of the Three: the battle of words, wits, and arms. He tells of the horror of the black mamba and how Hubris's arrogant celebration and pride brought his own defeat and explains that Hubris is forever banished to the great, cold North. He shares that when the storm blew, taking Hubris away, it also covered him with leaves, dirt, and twigs, protecting him from the light of day.

The questions go back and forth for another hour. Gillo says, "May I ask one last question?"

All answer, "Sure."

"How did you know which seeds were the cure and which were poison to trolls?"

"Hensley, how did you go about choosing the seeds?" asks the doctor with like curiosity.

"It was easy," says Hensley. "I just picked the smallest seeds. I figured that Gillo was small, everyone's hope was small, and our chances seemed small. So the obvious choice was the smallest seeds."

Gillo laughs and says, "Is not the trust and reasoning of a child's innocence a precious gift? Do I not see that the hour is getting late in my room? Shall you not return to your room and realm? Do I not ask that our friendship be ours alone and not to be known to others? Is it not true that if my presence be known, I would have to flee Newburg?"

All agree and give their word of secrecy. The doctor rises first and bids all that it is time to say their good-byes and return to the house.

"Am I not grateful for our visit? Do I also not bid you adieu, adieu?"

When all return to the house and walk down the stairs, they hear the clock chime the "Westminster Quarters" and strike once. It is 6:15. Only fifteen minutes have passed since they left the dining room. They laugh and share their experience, often with everyone talking at the same time.

## Christmas with Gillo

How can things get any better? Sue has a real, live troll doll. Hensley has his best friend, and the entire family has the most delightful house guest for Christmas. The children are off for Christmas vacation. The snow is falling. And the Wilson Manor has never been happier. The doctor always makes sure they find the tallest and fullest Christmas tree there is. Fortunately, the house has extremely high ceilings. The tree this year is twelve feet tall, and decorating it is joyous chaos: music playing, cookies baking, children laughing, pine needles falling, and boxes of decorations stacked high. And this year, a troll is there to help with the festivities. The tree always goes into the Tuscan Room due to its high ceilings and picture window facing the carriage house.

As everyone is busy opening boxes, decorating cookies, and doing all that goes with getting a house ready for Christmas, Grammy Cora says, "Who's playing the piano in the ladies' parlor?"

Great-Gram says, "Come—hurry. Look who's playing the piano."

They peek into the parlor, and there's Gillo, standing on the piano bench, playing "Jingle Bells" from one end of the keyboard to the other. His arms are stretched wide, and his four fingers are playing as if there are twelve on each hand. He looks over his shoulder and gives the biggest grin. "Is it good for me to play your piano, being that I do not have one in my tree?" he says as he keeps on playing. What a sight to see—an eight-inch piano player standing on the bench, running back and forth, playing with amazing zeal and skill. "Will you not join me and sing?" says Gillo.

And they do. It seems that the louder he plays, the louder they sing. It is as if they are playing a volume game. They sing all their favorite carols: "Jingle Bells," "O Christmas Tree," "What Child Is This?," "Deck the Halls," and many others.

Decorating the tree with Gillo is as fun as it gets. He decorates all around the bottom of the tree. He then climbs the tree and hangs the trinkets and candles where the family can't reach. To top it all off, he climbs to the tip top of the tree, lowers some twine, pulls the star up, and fastens it as high as can be. He then sits on top of the star and asks, "Can we sing 'Silent Night'?"

And they do; the song and the tree are beautiful. They all applaud, and Gillo bows with laughter.

No sooner do they finish singing than there is a knock on the side door, and then they hear, "Hello! Merry Christmas!" It is the neighbors, Paul and Mary. Before Gillo has a chance to climb down the tree, they are in the room.

"Oh, your tree is beautiful," says Mary.

Grammy Cora, being the hostess that she is, says what she always says when company arrives: "Please, have a seat. Let me get some coffee and cookies."

They all sit down, glancing at the tree and smiling to hide their wonder; where's Gillo? Hensley looks up and sees him hiding behind the star and peeking out with the biggest grin.

Suddenly, Gillo slips and falls. There he is, hanging from a branch upside down—again wearing that silly grin. Everyone sees him fall except Paul and Mary. They all gasp. Paul says, "Is everything all right? You all look like you've seen a ghost."

"Fine, fine—yes, sir, we're all fine, just fine," stammers the doctor. Then there is a crashing sound and a shout of "Woo!" This time, everybody looks at the tree, including Paul and Mary.

"What's that?" asks Paul.

"What? I didn't hear anything," answers the captain. The children giggle and cover their faces. "Oh, something just fell from the tree. It's nothing. Here's Cora with the coffee and cookies."

"Why don't we go into the parlor, where we can be more comfortable?" says Grammy Cora.

"Oh, no! Let's stay here; your tree is so beautiful. How in the world did you get the decorations all around and the star hung?" asks Mary.

Sue answers, "Gillo climbed the tree."

"Who's Gillo?" asks Paul with a look of wonder.

"Oh, you know children and their imaginary friends," answers the doctor.

"Would you like more coffee or cookies?" asks Grammy Cora.

Everyone looks at her with an expression of *We're hoping they go so that Gillo can come down out of the tree.* After a wonderful Christmas visit, Paul and Mary leave. The family members all show them to the door and say their good-byes. Sue says, "Adieu, adieu." The doctor just smiles and politely shuts the door.

They all run back into the Tuscan Room to check on Gillo. He comes walking out from under the tree, brushes himself off, looks up, smiles, and says, "Wow-we, wasn't that a close one?"

Naturally, Gillo is in his tree home during the daylight hours. Most of the family go to bed around nine. That gives them a few hours together in the evenings—they are treasured hours, filled with storytelling, Gillo playing the piano, and the family singing along. Gillo and the captain tell stories that are whoppers. They each have the ability to tell a true story in such colorful detail that even if you were there, it still sounds brand new.

For example, the captain tells a story one night that he believes he might have once been a troll. "Yes sirree, Bob, I was once under a foot tall. I would be up in the middle of the night often, scaring people. I could make the most horrible sounds, and people would come running, and when they got real close, I could make a stink worse than a skunk. I could make people laugh just by making funny sounds and faces. Yes, sir, I think I was once a troll."

Gillo laughs and says, "Does 'yes sirree, Bob' mean that's a tall tale? Is it not true that you were once only eight inches tall like me? Is it not also true that you could make people laugh and make them also cry because of the smell you would release? And is it not so that you are speaking about when you were a baby? Have I not seen your baby pictures? And were you not so ugly that maybe you were a troll?" Then Gillo laughs and rolls on the floor, holding his stomach and kicking his feet. Then everyone roars with laughter.

The family always goes to church on Christmas Eve. Everyone gets ready and is about to leave, when Grace sees Gillo sitting on a shelf in the doctor's library. "What are you doing, Gillo?" she asks.

"Is not Gillo shelved for the night? Will he not be fine?"

Grace gives him a pat on his head and leaves the room. She tells everyone in a whisper, "I think Gillo feels badly that he can't go to church with us."

"Oh yes," says Mary. "We can just walk into church with a troll on Christmas Eve. I don't think that is such a good idea."

Great-Gram says, "I've got an idea." She walks over to the sofa and empties her purse. "I can put him in my purse and just leave the top open."

Everyone stares at her. The captain says, "Hey, why not? Go get the little guy."

Grace goes back to the library. "Gillo, would you like to go to church with us?"

"Is it not cruel to tease Gillo about such things?"

Grace smiles and tells Gillo the plan. He climbs down from the shelf and runs and jumps into Great-Gram's purse with the biggest smile ever. Gram says, "Oh my, he's heavier than I thought. Captain, will you carry my purse?"

The captain rolls his eyes and says, "Give me the bag."

"It's not a bag; it's a purse," says Great-Gram.

"I know it's a purse; I'm referring to Gillo."

"Is the man with the purse calling me a bag?" There is, as always with Gillo, more laughter.

It's a beautiful, snowy Christmas Eve. There are candles in the windows of the church, and it is filled with people. The family walks in, and fortunately, only the back row is available. Gillo had closed the purse to keep the snow off. They sit down, and there's that gruff voice: "Hey, will somebody unzip this thing?"

The congregation begins singing Christmas carols, and Gillo decides to sing along. Gillo can do a lot of things well, but singing isn't one of them. People keep looking back to where the family is sitting, hearing this off-tune, gruff voice singing as loudly as it can. The captain pretends that it is him singing and just smiles at the people turning around to look. It is a memorable Christmas Eve service.

They return home. It is a Christmas Eve tradition for a family member to read the Christmas story. Hensley asks, "'How about we have Gillo read the story tonight?'"

He does so, and he does it from memory. He begins by quoting Isaiah 9:6 in is gruff but kind voice: "'For unto us a Child is born, unto us a Son is given; and the government will be upon His shoulder. And His name will be called Wonderful, Counselor, Mighty God, Everlasting Father, Prince of Peace.'" And he adds, "'Of the increase of His government and peace there will be no end.'" And then he recites the story from Matthew 1:18–2:23, word for word.

The captain says, "In my nearly ninety-four years, I've never heard it done so well." Everyone stands and applauds.

Naturally, Gillo, never missing an opportunity to be the showman, takes a deep bow and says, "'Twas it not 'The Night before Christmas,'[63] and do we not say, 'Happy Christmas to all, and to all a good night'? And furthermore, may I say adieu, adieu?"

---

[63] Poem by Clement Clarke Moore, 1822, "'Twas the Night before Christmas."

## — Chapter 10 —
# Then There Is Trouble

We need never be ashamed of our tears.
—Charles Dickens, *Great Expectations*

hristmas Day is glorious. It is a white Christmas. Everyone is healthy. The family waits until nightfall before they exchange gifts so that Gillo will be able to take part. There are the usual gifts: sweaters and socks, ties and shirts, candies and toys. Gillo has a gift for all: To the doctor, he gives the books from *Charity*; to the captain, he gives his seeds (they are white rose seeds); to Hensley, he gives his compass (which he has repaired); to Mary, Grace, and Sue, he gives necklaces made from quartz and gemstones from the old Newburg mines; and to Great-Gram and Grammy Cora, he gives his silver-and-gold cutlery.

The family has a great surprise for Gillo. "Gillo, we have a surprise for you. It's in the barn," says Hensley.

They all put on their coats and hats and trudge through the snow to the barn. The family is so excited to give Gillo his gift that they forget that the snow is too deep for him to walk in. They arrive at the barn, and Sue asks, "Where's Gillo?"

They look back toward the house, and all they see is his hat sticking out of the snow. Hensley runs back and helps him. He shakes his head and says, "Is not Gillo a snowman?"

Grace makes Gillo wear a blindfold. They open the barn, light the kerosene lamps, and walk Gillo in. "Okay," says Hensley, "on three, take off the blindfold—one, two, three."

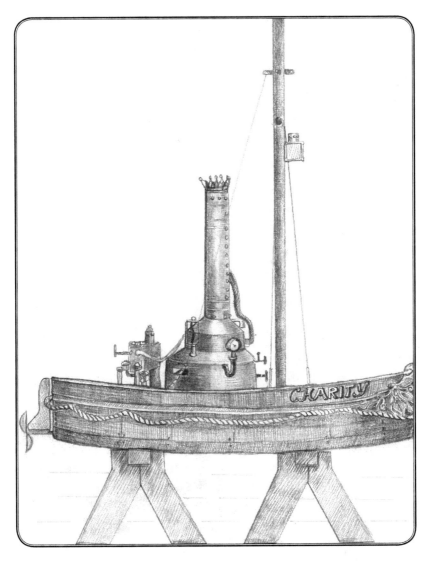

Gillo removes his blindfold and stands there, speechless. He doesn't move or speak a word for what seems to be forever. He walks up to his gift, gently touches it, and walks around it. He climbs up on it and turns to the family. "Does not Gillo now believe in miracles? How can this be? Is this not impossible?" The biggest tears roll from his eyes—too big for such a small troll. "How does Gillo say thank you? Where, how did you find it?" Everyone else is also in tears. The gift is Gillo's riverboat, *Charity*.

"Do you remember the story of Alex Moore and me finding it in the tree by the river?" says the captain. "I thought that it had washed away, but Alex had it hidden in his barn all these years. He passed away a few months ago, and his wife, Carol, asked me if I would like to have it. I've been working on it for Hensley. I was planning on giving it to him this Christmas. When I showed it to him, he didn't hesitate. He immediately said, 'This belongs to Gillo. We've got to give it to him. That would be my greatest Christmas present ever.'"

## Something Fishy

"There's something fishy going on at the Wilson Manor. I'm sure of it," says Mr. Lewis, the postman. "Now, I'm not one to repeat gossip, so I'm only going to say this once: I heard that Dr. Cola and the captain have found some kind of treasure and are hiding it."

"That's nonsense," says Mary. "We've been their neighbors for years. They are honest and good people."

When Mr. Lewis leaves, Paul says, "You know, Mary, when we were visiting the doctor and Cora for Christmas, didn't you think that they all acted a little strange?"

Mary says, "Now, Paul, you're sounding like that gossiping mailman, Tim Lewis."

"Mary, he does know what's going on in Newburg. He sees everyone's post and knows just about everybody's business. I know that our neighbors are good people, but they sure have been acting odd lately. Carol Moore told me the other day about her poor dead husband, Alex. God rest his soul. He and the doctor found a mysterious box or something about the time the story of the Troll of Newburg was going around."

"Now, Paul, that's an old, silly story that took place over ninety years ago."

"One never knows about this kind of thing—no, ma'am, one never knows," says Paul.

"Now, I have noticed that they have been drawing their curtains in the evening," says Mary in a wondering voice. "Paul, I think we should pay the doctor and Cora a visit and let them know that some folks are talking. They're not only our neighbors; they're our very good friends."

That evening, Paul and Mary, as good friends and neighbors should do, go to tell their friends of the latest talk of the town. Cora answers the door with "Paul, Mary, please come on in. How good to see you. It sure has been a busy Christmas season, hasn't it?" They return the cordial greeting and ask if they may speak with the doctor and her. "Sure, let me get Joseph. Come into the parlor."

"Good evening, Paul, Mary. Cora said that you would like to chat with us. Is everything all right? Is there some problem?"

Mary tells them what Mr. Lewis has said and that others have also been talking. The doctor and Cora look at each other, and the doctor speaks. "Paul, you and Mary have been trusted friends for a long time. We would hate to keep anything from you. We have been wonderful neighbors for too long. Can you wait here for just a minute or two? I'll be right back."

The doctor goes into the Tuscan Room, where the children have been playing a board game with Gillo, who is now hiding. When the neighbors came in, Gillo stepped behind a chair. He's fairly easy to hide. "Gillo," says the doctor, "we've got a little problem."

Gillo, in his never-ending humor, says, "I know I'm small, Doctor, but do you have to refer to me as a little problem?"

After some laughter, the doctor says, "Gillo, I'm serious. Paul and Mary have been dear friends and neighbors for decades. They know that something has changed in our home. I also know that it is a bit troublesome for people to know about you. Nevertheless, we just can't keep you from them. I would like to introduce you to them; would that be okay with you?"

Gillo says, "Do I not trust those you trust, and do I not love those you love? Shall we not be introduced to Paul and Mary, the neighbors?"

"That's great," says the doctor. "Wait here until I call for you, and, children, you can bring Gillo into the parlor."

"Okay, Grandfather," say all three.

"Paul, Mary, do you remember the story about the Troll of Newburg that took place, my, nearly a hundred years ago?" They just stare at the doctor. "I might as well skip all that; children, bring in our guest." Being the gracious and polite people Paul and Mary are, they stand to meet the guest. "Paul, Mary, this is Gillo."

Gillo steps out from behind the children. He bows, as always, almost touching his head to the floor, raises up, and says, "Is it not mighty fine to meet you, Mr. Paul and Mrs. Mary?" He then gives them his enormous troll smile.

Mary's eyes roll back, and she faints. Paul sits down and, without looking at Mary, fans her and says, "Mary, are you all right?"

Mary raises her head and sees Gillo again. He smiles and bows. She faints again. Mary finally regains her composure. She and Paul sit on the sofa. Gillo climbs up on the tea table so that they don't have to look down and says, "Would you like for me to play the piano and sing some songs?" Mary nearly faints again.

The doctor says, "Not right now, Gillo. Why don't you take the children back and finish the board game?"

Gillo bows and says, "Is it not good to meet you? May I bid you adieu, adieu?"

For the next hour or so, the doctor tells as much of the story as he thinks they can handle for one night. Then he says, in all firmness, "Paul, Mary, I have to ask that this stay between us. Can you imagine the trouble it would cause if word got out that there was a troll in Newburg?"

"We certainly understand. Your secret is our secret. We better be going. It's been a most interesting evening."

Paul and Mary keep their word and say not a word to anyone. Mr. Lewis, on the other hand, never stops talking about the goings-on at the Wilson Manor. Before long, people begin to walk by the house just to see if there is any truth to the rumors of treasure or the house being filled with trolls. Sue, in her childlike innocence, tells the other little neighborhood children that she has a live doll baby named Gillo. Grace and Hensley are mocked and made fun of at school. Things begin to be a bit quieter in the house. There isn't as much laughter. Everyone, including Gillo, becomes more serious.

One evening, as the doctor is in the kitchen, he happens to peer out the window and see someone with a pry bar trying to open the little door on the old maple tree. When the intruder sees the doctor watching, he runs away. It gets ugly in Newburg. If something is missing or damaged, the rumor mill blames the goings-on at the manor. When Great-Gram, Grammy Cora, or Mary are at the store, people who were once good friends just stare at them and whisper. The once-honored family of 221 Luna-Vista Avenue is now being shunned in their own hometown.

One day, after school, as Hensley is walking home, Peewee Jonson and Jake Brown corner him; Jake says, "We know that it must have been a bunch of those trolls living in your house that tossed us out of the Moore barn last fall. We know where you live. You better watch out. We're not afraid of you or your trolls."

Hensley does not know what to do. Neither does the rest of the family, nor does Gillo. Gillo, like all good trolls, is terribly naive. They never stop believing in the good of people; they never stop hoping, nor do they ever give up. In a word, they have charity.

The doctor calls for a family meeting. He begins, "We have a problem. All of us have experienced being harassed or shunned in the community. The rumors and gossiping are endless. Do we have a secret? Yes, we certainly have a secret. Is it anyone's business? No, it truly is no one else's business. Are we hiding a troll? Yes, we are. Is our reasoning just? I believe that it is."

Gillo is sitting on the piano bench sadly. He asks if he can speak. The doctor nods. "Am I not here to guard and protect those that I love? Have I not done so in my 187 years? Do I mean no harm? If I would be known, would it not be the end of my duty as a watchman and a helper? Am I not just a messenger of good news? What shall I do? Where shall I go? How do I rid you, my dear friends and my family, of these troubles? Is not Gillo truly sorry?" He places his face in his four-fingered hands and weeps bitterly. One and all rush to him and comfort him.

Great-Gram speaks as only a matriarch can. "Gillo, you are just as much a part of our family as any of us. We would no more ask you to leave or put yourself in harm's way any more than we would ask Sue or Hensley or anyone in this family to do so. We need you, and we hope that you need us."

The captain says, "We need a plan. There is to be no untruthfulness. Yet there are some things that are not to be revealed. When asked if we have a troll living with us, answer, 'Yes, the captain thinks that he was once a troll.'" There are smiles and small laughter. "If asked whether or not we have any treasure, say, 'Yes, the captain found an old boat when he was a young boy and still has it.' During the daylight hours, when Gillo is in his house or wherever he goes, live your lives as you have always done. Be friendly; be good neighbors. Paul and Mary have sure been good neighbors to us. To my knowledge, they have not said a word. Grace and Hensley, study hard in school. If someone makes fun of you with regard to trolls, ask them, 'What does a troll look like? I'll sure be keeping an eye out for one.'" There is a little more laughter, and even Gillo give his big grin.

"That settles it," says the doctor. "Just like *The Three Musketeers*[64]: 'One for all, and all for one.'"

Gillo laughs and says, "Shall I not get my sword?"

## Trouble Turns to Tragedy

We can easily forgive a child who is afraid of the dark;
The real tragedy of life is when men are afraid of the light.
—Plato[65]

For the next several days, there is a severe winter storm. It rains and snows; the temperature falls well below freezing and then climbs, causing the snow and ice to melt. The Moon River has crested far above flood stage. Newburg is nearer being flooded than any time in its long history. The rain and snow are relentless. Even the captain remarks that he has never seen the river so high. Foolishly, a few of the townsfolk blame the Troll of Newburg, now being called the Troll of Wilson Manor. The inclement weather is making everyone a little short-tempered and angry. If the rain and snow stop for even a few minutes, folks go out and patch roofs and check the rising of the river. School has been cancelled for days. The children have cabin fever.[66] A child can play only so many board games, color so many pictures, and read so many books. "Children," the captain says, "were made to be outside playing and getting dirty. A clean child is a bored child."

Peewee Jonson and Jake Brown have had enough of the boredom of the storm and think it is time for a little fun. After the storm, the snow has become hard and more ice than snow. It makes the hardest snowballs—good for throwing but not good for playing. Being the hurtful boys that they are, throwing ice balls at birds and dogs is their idea of fun. As they are walking

---

[64] A novel by Alexandre Dumas, first serialized in March–July 1844.

[65] Plato was a philosopher in classical Greece, born in 428 BC.

[66] Restlessness resulting from long confinement indoors during the winter.

down Luna-Vista, they come to Hensley Addison's house. It is fairly early in the morning, and they don't see anyone around.

"Hey, Jake," Peewee says, "let's snowball Hensley's house."

Jake says, laughing, "What if the troll gets us?" They cross the street on the river side and make an arsenal of iced snowballs. "Okay, on three, let's let 'er have it—one, two, three!"

The snowballs fly. Suddenly, there is a crash of shattering glass; Jake has hit the parlor window, and it has exploded into smithereens. When the doctor hears the crash, he runs to the front of the house and onto the porch. When Jake and Peewee see him, they take off running. Peewee runs down the street toward home, but for some reason, Jake runs over the hill, toward the river. The captain, who was also having coffee in the kitchen, helps the doctor clean up the broken glass and patch the open window. While they are mending the damage, they hear a child calling for help. Not sure from where the sound is coming, they walk around the house and strain to hear from which direction it comes.

The doctor hurriedly walks across the street and looks over the hill, and to his shocked disbelief, there is Jake, hanging on a tree that has been uprooted from the riverbank. As the doctor is running and skidding down the hill in his slippers and house jacket, the tree suddenly breaks loose. Jake, still holding on to its branches, is quickly swept away in the torrent.

A few of the neighbors come to see what all the fuss is. The doctor runs along the riverbank to see if there is any way to help the screaming boy, but the water is too swift, and Jake has washed out into the middle of the raging river. Before long, a crowd has gathered, murmuring, "What happened? Whose boy is it?"

Peewee comes running up with his father, confessing to having thrown the snowballs with Jake Brown. "Someone go get Mrs. Brown!" calls the doctor. Mr. Brown, unfortunately, is a drunkard and spends most of his days in one of the town taverns.

Mrs. Brown is, naturally, frantic with grief and worry. "My

boy—someone get him, please! Someone help him!" He is out of sight.

The captain says, "There is no way that we can get a boat in that river. The only hope is that he runs into Green's Island. It's a good two miles downriver. He is probably already there by now."

A few of the men walk along the river, looking for the child. The doctor tells the captain, "Dad, that boy cannot last long in that ice-cold water. Unless we are able to do something real soon, I'm afraid there's no hope."

By then, Grammy Cora and Great-Gram have Mrs. Brown in the kitchen with Mary. They are doing their best to comfort her.

Hensley asks the doctor, "Grandfather, is there anything I can do? Jake isn't a bad boy. He just doesn't have anyone to teach him right from wrong."

Peewee is crying, saying, "It's all my fault."

Hensley comforts him and says, "No, Peewee, it was an accident. I know that you didn't purposefully break the window, and Jake just made a mistake. Everything that can be done will." Hensley runs into the house and gets the key to the seventh door. He runs down the long corridor to Gillo's door and knocks loudly.

Gillo comes quickly. "What is it? Is something wrong?" Hensley explains quickly what has happened. "Should you not return?" says Gillo. "Should not I weigh the problem?"

Hensley goes back to be with Peewee. It seems that all hope is lost. Surely Jake cannot survive long in the raging, cold river. A crowd has gathered in front of the house. All eyes are on the river. Suddenly, someone yells, "Look! It's a little boat."

The crowd turns and sees a small boat on a wagon with smoke puffing from its stack, moving on the walkway toward the street. The crowd is even more stunned when they see Gillo pulling the wagon. The captain orders everyone to clear the way. Gillo has a determined look. He doesn't look to the left or right. He looks straight ahead.

"It's the troll—the Troll of Newburg!" someone yells.

Hensley says, "No, it is the gatekeeper of Newburg. His name is Gillo. He will rescue Jake. Please clear the way."

Everyone stands aside, forming two rows of people. It seems that the whole town is there. Not a word is spoken as Gillo passes. Men remove their hats. Ladies give a slight curtsy. When Gillo has pulled the wagon near the top of the hill facing the river, he climbs aboard and says to Hensley, "Will you be my first mate and shove me off?" Hensley nods and gives the little boat and wagon a push. Over the hill, the boat flies.

Gillo stands at the helm with his face toward the river. He looks taller and nobler than ever. The boat plunges into the raging river, and with a huge puff of smoke and a clanking of the steam engine, off he goes downstream. He is soon out of sight. Mrs. Brown comes out of the house and stands along the hillside with the rest of the folks of Newburg. Time passes slowly. On top of it all, it begins to rain again, and a fog moves in on the river. The shore is barely visible. No one leaves.

All stand in the rain with their eyes on the riverbank. Hensley yells, "Listen! I think I hear a boat." The crowd is still and quiet. For a moment, the only noise is the tender weeping of Mrs. Brown. Then they hear the little steam engine straining and clanging as it pushes against the charging current. The sound of the little boat's whistle echoes in the air: *whooa-whooa*. "It must be Gillo's boat," says Hensley. "He's looking to land the boat. We need a lantern."

Grace comes running with a lantern, and some of the men run over the hill. So does Hensley, against the wishes of his mother. The men wave the lamp, and the captain shouts, "Ahoy, Gillo, ahoy!"

Through the fog, they begin to see Gillo's tiny boat. Lying across the bow is the limp body of Jake. Gillo tosses a line, and the men grab it and pull the boat ashore. The doctor grabs Jake, covers him with a blanket, and climbs the hill as fast as he can. He brings Jake into the house and, a few minutes later, comes out and says, "He's going to be all right. He just has some bruises, and he's mighty cold, but he'll be fine. His mom is with him."

"Gillo! Where's Gillo?" calls Hensley. In the excitement of getting Jake, no one paid attention to the boat or Gillo. Hensley and Peewee run over to the hillside, and lo and behold, there is Gillo, pulling the wagon and boat up the hill. He is soaked to the bone and looks like a wet cat.

"Are you not to be concerned about Gillo? Has he not pulled his boat alone many times?"

The crowd applauds as Gillo pulls the boat across the street. Someone yells, "Speech—give us a speech!"

Gillo looks at Hensley and the doctor, and they give nods of approval. Gillo climbs upon the banister of the porch as everyone gathers around. He gives a huge grin and bows, almost falling off the banister. Everyone laughs; after all, he is a sight—all chubby eight inches of him. In his gruff voice, he says, "Are you not the good people of the fine town of Newburg? Am I not called Gillo? Have I not been in your town for nearly one hundred years? Have I not been able to hide and go about doing the good that I can without being seen? Have I not this day done what any of you would have done if you had a boat like mine? Are you not to be most grateful to the great Captain Jaeger? Was it not him who rescued my boat and repaired it for such a time as this? Do you not owe this wonderful family an apology for doing nothing more than being hospitable to a creature like me? In their graciousness, will they not say, 'No apology needed'? Is not Gillo mighty cold, and is he not being exposed to the daylight? So is it not time for me to say thank you and adieu, adieu?" The crowd whistles and applauds as Gillo smiles and bows and once again almost falls off the banister. Gillo hurries to his tree home so that he doesn't shrink or crack any more.

That evening, a nonstop flow of people walks by the house, hoping to get a glimpse of the Troll of Newburg. About eight that evening, there is a hard knock on the door. The doctor goes to see who's visiting at this hour. Mr. and Mrs. Brown and Jake are at the door. Mr. Brown, quite haggard looking and disheveled, says, "I hear that someone here saved my son's life. If that's so, I just want to shake his hand and say thanks for saving the kid."

For the sake of Mrs. Brown and Jake, the doctor invites them in. "Please have a seat in the parlor."

Grammy Cora comes into the room and hugs Mrs. Brown and asks if they would like something to drink. Mrs. Brown and Jake say, "No, thank you."

Mr. Brown says, "I'll have a beer if you got any."

"I'm sorry, Mr. Brown; we do not have any beer. Would you care for an iced tea or water?" asks Cora.

"Na, thanks anyway," answers Mr. Brown. It is obvious that Mr. Brown is still a slight bit inebriated.

The doctor returns to the parlor. "Mr. Brown, this is Gillo; he is the one who rescued Jake."

Mr. Brown stands up, a little wobbly, and says in a slurred voice, "Well, where is he?"

"Isn't it nice to make your acquaintance, Mr. Brown?" Gillo sticks out his hand.

Mr. Brown looks down, falls back on the sofa, and, in a sobering voice, says, "I'm done. That's it—no more. I'm never taking another drink."

"Would you not agree, Mr. Brown, that no more drinking is a good idea?" says Gillo.

"Well, I'll be. Mr. Gillo, you sure ain't much for elevation. But I sure do truly thank you for saving my son." He shakes Gillo's hand. He then looks at Mrs. Brown and says, "I've not been a very good husband to you or father to Jake. But I truly believe that something just happened to me after meeting this little fella, Mr. Gillo. With the Good Lord's help, I will stay sober."

Mr. Brown never did take another drink; he stayed sober and became an upstanding citizen and a loving husband and father for the remainder of his days.

# — Chapter 11 —
# Growing Older without Growing Up

Don't try to make me grow up before my time.
—Louisa May Alcott, *Little Women*, 1868

or a season, everything is beyond wonderful. Grace and Hensley are extremely popular at school. They are actually famous not only in Newburg but also in Mill's Fort and Bedford Falls. The girls who once were mean and cruel to Grace welcome her as a true friend. People pass 221 Luna-Vista with smiles and wave, mostly hoping to get a glimpse of the Troll of Newburg. Gillo becomes a celebrity. His picture is in all the newspapers.

Popularity is an enjoyable thing, but mostly it is short lived. It is based not on who you are inside but on who people think you are on the outside. It is usually, if not always, short-lived fame.

It doesn't take long for both Grace and Hensley to learn that their popularity is conditional. The kids want to see Gillo, and if that isn't going to happen, then their popularity fades. As Gillo can never be seen during the daylight hours, his accessibility is very limited; plus, he is terribly shy. Trolls, by nature, are solitary beings. Gillo is somewhat of an exception to the rule. He is a one-family troll.

Months and then years pass. There is little talk about the Troll of Newburg. He is forgotten by many. Grace has graduated from high school and is finishing college in Mill's Fort. Hensley is about to begin his high school years, and Sue is finishing her elementary years. The captain is about to celebrate his one hundredth birthday. He and Great-Gram are as healthy as ever, still full of life and stories. Grammy Cora and the doctor are enjoying their lives. They normally spend their evenings with Gillo, more so than the children. School and friends have a way of replacing family time.

It is often a sight, seeing the doctor and Gillo sitting in the library reading, the doctor at his writing desk and Gillo sitting in the rocking chair with a book as big as him.

Occasionally, people stop and ask if this is the house where the troll lives and if they can have a picture taken with him; most of the time, Gillo obliges with his huge smile.

Things have changed. The passing of time has a way of doing that. Friends we have as children most likely will not be the friends we have as adults. Relationships change, as do people. I think we call that growing up.

As time continues to pass, Gillo becomes less and less visible. There are times that he isn't seen for days on end. When asked why, he kindly answers, always with that big smile, "Does not Gillo have errands to run and problems of government to solve?"

## Thanksgiving

Nothing is more honorable than a grateful heart.
—Seneca[67]

It is the family's best Thanksgiving Day ever. They obviously wait until evening so that Gillo can join them. As always, there are guests. Grace is home from college, and Mr. and Mrs. Brown and Jake join them, along with Paul and Mary and the postman, Mr. Lewis (all has been forgiven). They have to extend the dining

---

[67] Roman Stoic philosopher, 4 BC–AD 65.

room table to accommodate everyone. Oh, the smells that come from the kitchen. Everyone takes part.

It is hilarious to see Gillo carrying trays of food; they can only see the trays and hear his gruff voice: "Should you not excuse me? Am I not coming through?"

After everyone is seated, the doctor asks, "Gillo, would you mind pronouncing the blessing?"

They hold hands as Gillo prays. "Are we not so truly thankful for all the blessings of life? Do we not give thanks for family and friends, neighbors, and even trolls? And oh, are we not so very thankful for all this food that we are about to devour? Do we not all say together, 'Amen'?" And they eat. And they laugh. And they eat some more and laugh even more. It is a terrific Thanksgiving dinner. Yes, they are thankful.

After dinner, they all share the things they are thankful for. Mr. Lewis starts. "I am thankful for forgiveness. I talked about things I assumed to be true and were not."

Mr. Brown says, "I am so thankful for my wife and son and these years of sobriety."

Paul and Mary hold hands, and Paul says, "We are thankful for each other, for our family who are away, and for our neighbors inviting us to dinner."

The captain says, "I am thankful for my wife of seventy-five years and my children and grandchildren and great-grandchildren and, I hope, soon-coming great-great-grandchildren."

Grammy Cora says, "I am thankful for the blessings of our family and home, the good days, and even the difficult ones. God has been good to us."

Grace says she is thankful to be home for Thanksgiving. Sue gives thanks for friends and family.

Hensley says, "I am thankful for each and every one at our table, especially my friend—who some thought to be my imaginary friend—Gillo."

The doctor says, "Yes, we sure all have a lot to be thankful for. Gillo, you are the last but obviously not the least. For what are you thankful?"

Gillo, with permission, stands on the table; he then bows, smiles, and looks at each person, especially Hensley, and says, "I am ..." He pauses for the longest time, takes a deep breath, and continues.

"I am thankful that I no longer have to speak with questions. I now can say what I know to be true, honest, and of a good report."

Everyone is amazed to hear Gillo speaking without asking a question. He has everyone's full attention. He goes on. "I am thankful that I have learned what true love is. This family has taught me that love is patient and kind. You are never jealous of others; you do not brag, nor are you prideful. You have always honored me and have never been selfish. You were never angry with me, nor did you keep a record of my wrongdoings. You did not like that evil Hubris; nevertheless, you did not hate him—you only hated the things he did. You always sought the truth. You have always protected, trusted, and endured me and my silliness. Your hope in me never stopped, nor has your love ever failed. You have always welcomed strangers into your home, me being the most strange. You never judged me for my size or others for their color. I am so thankful that I have been honored to watch over this family for nearly a century. Captain, you helped me—or should I say that I helped you with the saintly Harriet Tubman? Hensley Addison, I am so thankful that you have believed in me. Because of your belief when others did not believe, I have been gifted to be seen and known. I spoke with questions because I only knew in part, but now I know, just as I have become fully known. When I was a lonely troll, I talked like a troll, I thought like a troll, and I reasoned like a troll. When I met you, I became a person; I put my troll ways behind me. I am thankful that I have learned from you faith, hope, and love. Because of the greatness of that love, it is time for me to bid you, one and all, adieu, adieu."

For more information, and to experience *A Year with Gillo*
visit www.discoverthebible.com

CPSIA information can be obtained at www.ICGtesting.com
Printed in the USA
LVOW13*1256111113

360809LV00002B/11/P